The Shotgun Kid

Bill Carter, the tough boss of the Trouble J ranch, was doomed to meet his Maker as he was prodded into a fight and murdered by Lye Spar the *segundo* of Mervyn Judson who owned the town and most of the local cattle-country. Now it was down to Frank Carter the young, crippled son and his friend Lafe Kramer.

But there was worse to come for Judson had got hold of the Trouble J land and Frank and Lafe had just seven days to clear out. The boys weren't prepared to take it lying down and so began a vicious range war. Lafe was a hard hombre and Frank, crippled though he was, soon became known as the *Shotgun Kid* so deadly was he with the weapon.

With all the odds lined up against the pair, a bad case of lead poisoning looked like the only future they had.

The Shotgun Kid

Josh Richards

A Black Horse Western

ROBERT HALE · LONDON

© 1951, 2003 Vic J. Hanson
First hardcover edition 2003
Originally published in paperback as
The Shotgun Kid by V. Joseph Hanson

ISBN 0 7090 7261 9

Robert Hale Limited
Clerkenwell House
Clerkenwell Green
London EC1R 0HT

X000 000 006 8761

Typeset by
Derek Doyle & Associates, Liverpool.
Printed and bound in Great Britain by
Antony Rowe Limited, Wiltshire

ONE

Carter was still travelling fast when he hit the batwings. His heavy body split them apart leaving them swinging crazily. His heels shrieked on the boardwalk then kicked the air as he went over backwards. He finished up in the dust – beneath the speculative gaze of a grey mare at the hitching-rack.

Judson and Spar followed him out. They were both lean, mean-looking. Judson was the taller and older, the boss. His heavy black moustache accentuated the length of his jaw. Spar was whip-like, his wedge-shaped face yellow, his eyes small, shiny-black, like a sidewinder's.

Carter, resting on his left elbow, looked up at them. His face was lined and old, his fading blue eyes filled now with pain and hate. Crazily, he went for his gun.

Judson did not move. He did not have to. Spar drew with a flick of his wrist, firing as the muzzle cleared the leather. Carter belched as the slug hit him. His blue eyes were surprised. Then the light faded from them. They went blank. His arm straightened, and he lay down in the dusty, cart-rutted street as if he was dog-tired and couldn't wait to get his feet up.

There was a shuffling and a muttering from the folks whose faces stuck above the batwings.

Judson turned. 'You all saw that, didn't yuh? Self-defence. Lye beat him to it.'

Lye Spar slid his gun back into its sheath. 'Yeah, it wuz him or me. The ol' buzzard meant to kill me all right.'

He whirled swiftly, hand dipping again as boot-heels clattered on the boardwalk.

'Hold it,' said Judson.

A kid ran into the road and threw himself down by the still form of Carter.

'Pa! Pa!'

He tried awkwardly to lift the grey head. He was a cripple – his right arm contorted, the hand minus three fingers. Looking into the dead face, realizing he could not do anything for his father now, he bent his head. A strangled sob shook his frail body.

He looked up suddenly, blue eyes blazing at the two men above him. His left hand groped for the gun in his father's belt.

Spar moved. 'Lye,' yelled Judson warningly. He left the sidewalk in a bound and kicked out at the kid.

He missed as the kid backed, the gun out, wavering to draw level. He swung again. The heavy boot crashed against the side of the kid's head. He crumpled, blood staining his face. He lay still a few yards from his father's body. The gun landed a foot or more away from his good hand. His withered right arm was crumpled beneath him.

Judson spoke out of the corner of his mouth. 'You'd better ride back to the ranch, Lye, jest in case. I guess Lafe Kramer's in town, too. I'll fix everythin'.'

Spar nodded. He forked his horse at the hitching-rack and rode off.

Mervyn Judson stood erect on the sidewalk, in his black cut-away coat, his pin-stripes tucked in fancy riding-boots. He turned to the watchers and shrugged. 'Lye cain't fight the whole Trouble J,' he said.

They were coming out on the sidewalk now. He said to them: 'Mebbe a few of you'll pick up these two an' bring 'em inside. The kid's only knocked out. One of yuh fetch Sheriff Budd.'

'Here he is already,' said somebody.

An enormously broad man came down the street. His long grey hair curled around his ears from beneath a battered Stetson. He raked the crowd with slit grey eyes in a mass of wrinkles in his hard, lined face. They parted to let him through to the two sprawling forms in the dust.

'Bill Carter!' he said. 'Young Frank!'

'The kid's only stunned,' said one lounger helpfully.

The sheriff ignored him. He was looking at the body of one of his oldest friends, the wide red stain on the breast of his shirt, drying in the hot sunshine.

But his grey eyes had lost their sadness as he looked up at Mervyn Judson, The tall man met the sheriff's gaze with a level one of his own, his poker face grave.

He said: 'Lye Spar shot it out with him. Self-defence. I reckon if Lye hadn't a' bin there I'd've got it. The ol' man was gunnin' fer me all right. An' yuh know I'm no gunman. The kid throwed down on us – I had to kick him side o' the haid.'

'Where is Spar?'

'He rode back tuh the ranch. Lafe Kramer and them other Trouble J boys are in town. Yuh know they're hard cases, Sheriff. Lye couldn't fight 'em all. We don't want a range war on our hands.'

Old Sheriff Budd's hard eyes raked the other's poker face, the heavy black moustache that slashed it in half. He said 'You told Spar tuh ride?'

Judson nodded. 'Yeah. I didn't want any more trouble.'

The sheriff turned to the crowd. 'Who saw all this?'

Most of them, habitual barflies of Judson's Curly Cat Saloon behind them, volunteered it was self-defence, just like Merv said. Carter had been a cantankerous old cuss, openly scornful of the 'town-softies' and, consequently, not overpopular here in Georgetown.

One old-timer piped up: 'I guess he wus kinda provoked, though.'

'Yeah?' said the sheriff interrogatively.

The other, an old desert-rat, avoided Judson's eyes and said: 'Merv knocked him through the batwings. I gotta be fair. I guess Carter was provoked. Though,' he added doubtfully, 'I guess he asked fer it in the fust place.'

Judson broke in: 'He wuz spoilin' for a fight. Threatened tuh blow me apart. I had to hit him.'

'Wal, we'd better go to the office an' hear it all,' said Sheriff Budd. 'You come along, old-timer; an' you, Judson. Some of yuh bring ol' Bill an' the kid along.'

Judson said: 'I don't see any reason why I should—'

The sheriff interrupted him. 'I'm takin' you in.'

'What for?'

'Accessory after the fact. You shouldn't've told Spar to ride. Chief witness.' Sheriff Budd shrugged. 'Anything you like. You're comin'.' His thumb was hooked in his belt, very close to the black-scarred butt of his low-slung gun.

Judson shrugged, too. 'All right, Joe. I know Bill Carter wuz a pard o' yourn,' he added maliciously.

'Whether or not, I'd still take you in.'

The crowd was getting thicker. A ripple ran through it. 'Let us through,' said a harsh voice. 'Goddam it! Let us through!'

The ranks parted. Three men strode into the inner ring where others were picking up the bodies of the dead man and the unconscious kid.

'Lafe, Jim, Olly,' said Sheriff Budd, by way of greeting. His voice held a warning note.

Lafe Kramer, the Trouble J straw-boss, carried himself like a prize-fighter, on his toes, shoulders hunched a little, long arms dangling. His saturnine face was dark, thin-lipped, his eyes hard. Right now they glowed with passion.

'The boss,' he said. 'Where is he?'

'He's dead, Lafe,' said Sheriff Budd flatly. 'Gun-fight with Lye Spar. Self-defence, they reckon.'

Then Kramer saw the body. 'Bill,' he said. 'An' Frank! What's happened tuh the kid?'

'Jest unconscious. He tried to start a war all on his lonesome.'

While the talk was progressing, Lafe Kramer's two pards were fanned out each side of him and a few steps behind. One was dark and blocky; the other, fair and lean. They looked hard customers. It was a formidable trio.

Kramer's eyes found the poker face of Mervyn Judson. He turned towards him.

'I reckon you had plenty to do with this. Where's Spar?'

'He rode outa town.'

'Convenient-like, eh?' jeered Kramer. 'You two didn't like the home-truths Bill came tuh tell yuh, eh? You long-faced buzzard!'

He took a step forward, his shoulders hunched a little more. His hands were claws, almost brushing the butts of his two guns.

Judson's face did not change expression, but it seemed to pale a little. Passion glowed in Kramer's eyes and gave a drawn look to his saturnine features. Boot-heels scraped as the crowd drew back. Kramer's pards, Jim and Olly, fanned out a little more, their bodies tensed, their eyes watchful.

'Hold it!' It was the harsh voice of Sheriff Budd that cracked out.

Kramer stood like an ominous statue. But his pose had undergone a subtle change. He was waiting now.

'It don't do to go off half-cocked, Lafe, an' kill the first person who comes tuh mind. That won't help ol' Bill none – or Frank. I'm takin' Judson in, an' I want no interference.'

Kramer began to back-pedal, still keeping his eyes on

the saloon-owner. Nothing in his manner gave any clue to what he meant to do. His pards stood and waited. The sheriff waited, his face grim, hoping. The little knot of people in the centre of the ring were like statues as Kramer stopped pacing. He was beside the sheriff.

He said: 'All right, Joe.' Then he moved. 'Come on, boys.'

The three of them burst through the crowd and ran for their horses.

'Don't start anything you'll regret, Lafe,' shouted the sheriff. 'Think!'

But he received no answer from the three Trouble J men as they rode down the street.

Young Frank Carter was moaning, his head rolling, as he began coming to. But they managed to get him into the Sheriff's office and lay him on the couch before he finally regained full consciousness.

'Pa,' he said, his blue eyes roaming around the little room. Then he saw Judson.

He sat up, pointing. 'He killed my pa!' he cried.

He rose to his feet, his eyes blazing now. His face was swollen and bloodied where the saloon-man had kicked it. He began to come nearer, his gammy arm pitifully crooked, but the other one bent, the hand balled into a fist.

'Take it easy, Frank,' said Sheriff Budd. 'If he did kill your dad he'll pay for it. But I gotta find out. All I know is that Lye Spar did th' shootin'. These folks are here to tell me more.'

But the kid was already going dizzy from the pain in his head; the intensity of his passion made him weak. Hank O'Toole, the big deputy, held on to him as he staggered, and led him back to the couch. He sat beside him, his bear-like arm around the thin shoulders.

In the office beside the kid, the deputy, the sheriff and Judson, were the old-timer who had spoken up outside, and the four men who had carried the bodies in. They had also seen the shooting. Old Bill Carter now lay in the room behind.

The sheriff looked worried. He was still wodering about Lafe Kramer and the other two Trouble J men. Things seemed to be boiling up into a real nasty situation. His lawman's brain struggled with his emotions as a man and a friend of the dead Bill Carter. He hated the poker-faced man with the thick black moustache who sat before him.

'All right, Judson,' he said harshly. 'Let's have your story first.'

The owner of the Curly Cat Saloon said: 'Carter came to see me on business.' He looked around at the assembled company. 'What the business was concerns nobody here at all.'

'I'll hear that later,' said the sheriff. 'Jest tell me what actually happened.'

'Wal, me an' Carter didn't see eye to eye on this business and he began to get abusive. You know what he's like when he's rattled. He threatened to get his boys and take my place apart, threatened to take me apart personally. I ordered him off the premises and sort of started to shepherd him to the door—'

'With the help of Lye Spar, no doubt?'

'Lye took no part in the conversation or anythin'. He kept behind me jest in case one of the Trouble J gunnies might've bin lurkin' around. We wuz by the batwings when Carter yelled: 'I'll blow yuh apart,' an' went for his gun. I hit him an' he went backwards through the batwings. I followed him out an' Lye must've come out behind me. Carter was getting up by the hitching-rail. He tried to draw again. Lye beat him to it. I guess I'd have bin a dead pigeon if he hadn't – you know my draw's no good, specially since I got my wrist busted.'

'So you keep sayin',' said the sheriff. He turned to the others.

One of them volunteered a statement pronto, even before he was asked. 'It was just like Merv tol' it, Sheriff. Carter was doin' a lotta blowin' an' threatenin'. Looked like he asked fer it.'

Others chimed in to corroborate that. The sheriff looked them over sardonically: maybe he ought to've let Judson speak last, so they wouldn't have had a lead to go on. Still, maybe he was being too suspicious – probably that was just how it did happen. He knew Bill Carter's temper; the old-timer hadn't been easy to get along with; Judson and Spar had seized their opportuhity and got rid of the old man who irritated and baulked them. The old sheriff thought he knew what was wrong, but he had a terrible feeling that there wasn't much he could do about it right now. Maybe he was getting too old. He twitched his shoulders – the biggest in the territory – looked at the garrulous old-timer who, strangely enough, was the only one who hadn't spoken yet.

'What do you say about it, Jake?'

'I tell it as I seed it,' said Jake, who was notorious for his forthrightness.

'Shoot,' said the sheriff.

'Wal, Bill Carter an' Merv here came outa Merv's office arguefyin' fit tuh bust. Lye Spar was standin' just outside, havin' a drink. He says somep'n to Bill as Bill passes him. There's a sneerin' sorta look on his pan. Bill turns on him, too. Then he's goin' away at both of 'em, callin' 'em all the skunks an' thieves – an' other things – he could lay his tongue to. Yuh know how he useter go off once he got started. Most times it wuz just hot air. This time though it looked kinda serious. He kept shakin' his fist under Merv's nose. Lye Spar wuz watchin' him like he wuz a stick o' dynamite. All of a sudden, Merv here yells: 'Get off my property!' – or words tuh that effect. Him an' Spar start tuh sort of shepherd Bill tuh the door. Bill keeps sayin' 'Yuh cain't get rid o' me like that,' but he keeps movin'. It looked like, although he was acting mighty het-up an' waving his arms about all the time, he didn't mean tuh let 'em force his hand. Then – when he wuz almost on top o'the batwings – Merv hit him—'

'Wait a minute!' said the sheriff. 'Did yuh see him go for his gun before Judson hit him?'

Jake shook his head emphatically. 'Nope! I wuz watchin' all of 'em. If things looked like getting stacked-up unevenlike, I wuz ready to help out.' He tapped his own gun in its shapeless, greasy holster. 'Nope, Bill didn't make a move in thet direction, his hands wuz up high most o' the time—'

'I tell yuh he went for his gun,' burst out Judson. 'He made an insulting remark then went for his gun.'

'I hate tuh contradict yuh, Merv,' said Jake politely. 'I wouldn't know about the insulting remarks – I guess most of what Bill Carter said could be looked upon as insulting – but I know he didn't reach for his gun—'

'Where wuz Spar at this time?' said Sheriff Budd.

'He wuz two–three steps behind Merv all the time.'

'Then what happened?'

'Merv an' Lye went through the batwings after Bill. Most of us followed.'

'What did yuh see?'

'Wal, I cain't move quite as fast as I useter,' said Jake. 'Some o' the young 'uns were there before me. I heard one shot. All I saw wuz Bill Carter lying back in the street. His hand was near his gun, so I guess he must've tried to draw. But he never had a chance against a fast *hombre* like Lye Spar.'

'If Lye hadn't've got him, the ol' buzzard would've got me,' said Judson.

'That's how it wuz,' said another man. 'Carter tried to throw down on 'em.'

'While he wuz still on the ground?'

'Yeah.'

'No wonder he didn't have a chance,' said the sheriff. His eyes bored into Judson. 'Wouldn't it've bin simpler tuh kick the gun out of his hand like you kicked young Frank up the chops?'

'I couldn't stop Lye shootin' the old man,' said Judson. 'He asked for it. But the kid couldn't defend himself so easily. I couldn't stand aside an' see him killed.'

'Very white of yuh! What did the kid do?'

'He got down an' reached for his old man's gun.'

'That right, Frank?'

'Yeah,' said the kid dully. 'They killed him like a dawg, Spar was just puttin' his gun back when I came. Pa's hand never reached his. He musta never had a chance to get up or nothin'—' The boy's voice broke.

The sheriff said brusquely: 'All right. All of yuh can go, except Judson. Thanks for the straight information, Jake.'

'You're welcome, Joe,' said the old-timer. 'Bill Carter wuz no pard o' mine, an, I got nothin' personally agin Merv Judson. But I like tuh see the law done right an' proper.' He filed out behind the other four men, leaving in the office young Frank Carter, Hank O'Toole, the sheriff, and the saloon-owner.

The latter said: 'Whadyuh want with me now, Joe?'

'I'm keepin' yuh here till we pick up your pal, Spar,' said the sheriff.

The black-moustached man bounded to his feet, his poker-face crumbling. 'Yuh cain't do that.'

Then he gulped at the gun that had appeared in Sheriff Budd's hand.

'Lock him up, Hank.'

The big deputy crossed the room and ran his hand expertly over Judson's clothing. He took a small, double-barreled derringer from the right hip-pocket of the black cut-away coat.

'Li'l sneakshooter,' he said, and tossed it on the desk.

'Come on, *Mister* Judson.'

As they passed Frank Carter, the kid looked up and said softly: 'You'd better stay locked up, Mister Judson.'

The old sheriff gave him a sharp glance from beneath beetling brows.

As the deputy and Judson passed through into the cell block, the latter called back: 'I demand tuh see Lawyer Markson.'

'I'll see Lawyer Markson for yuh,' said the sheriff drily.

'Tell him I'm bein' railroaded,' bawled Judson.

Sheriff Joe Budd bent his gaze on young Frank.

'It's Spar we really want, son,' he said.

'Yeah, I know, Sheriff.' The boy's voice was still dull, his eyes downcast, his whole pose indicative of his deep misery. And he probably felt his crippling incapacity now more than ever before.

The office door suddenly burst open and a youth of seventeen or so – about Frank's age – came in. It was the sheriff's son, Oakland. He was broad and muscular, like his father, his strong, good-looking face deeply tanned, his light-brown hair bleached white at the temples.

'Is that right?' he said. 'About Frank's dad?'

Then he saw Frank himself. 'It is,' he said. 'Oh, gosh. It was Judson an' Spar, wasn't it? The dirty sons!'

'Easy, Oak,' said his father.

'Yeah,' said the youth. He crossed the room and sat beside Frank. 'Have yuh got 'em, Dad?'

'We've got Judson in a cell. Spar high-tailed it. They plead self-defence – an' they got witnesses.'

'I don't doubt it,' said Oakland. His lips curled. He dropped a brown, muscular hand on Frank's good arm.

'We'll get 'em, pard,' he said. 'The dirty sons.'

'Easy, I said, Oak,' said his father sternly. His eyes were hooded as he looked at the two young friends. The one so strong and virile, a son to be proud of; the other a thin, sickly kid with a withered arm, a pinched face, with blue eyes like his father's – blue eyes that could flame like his father's used to. They'd seen some times together, Bill Carter and the sheriff. The old man shook off these thoughts and rose as Hank O'Toole appeared once more.

'We're riding after Spar.'

Both youths rose, too. The cripple's dull eyes flamed now.

The sheriff hesitated. Then he said: 'You'd better come along, Frank.' Truth was, he didn't like to leave the boy here with Judson so near and unarmed in the cell, and the armoury cupboard right close. 'Come on,' he said brusquely.

The sheriff turned as they reached the sidewalk. His son was following.

'You stay here, Oak,' the old man said. 'An' get Dry Dust.'

'Dry Dust' Weeks was the town's undertaker.

TWO

Lafe Kramer rode hard. His two pards rode one each side of him. The companionable rhythm of the three of them was like well-oiled machinery.

Jim McDougal was fair and lean, Olly Masters dark – blocky, like a solid, knotty chunk of pine.

The mesa around them was flat, a shimmering bluey-green haze under the blazing sun. It merged with the sky in a fluctuating line that was the horizon. The sun played queer tricks, flashing multi-coloured lights into the squinting eyes of the hard-riding men. The sweat ran down from beneath their hat-bands, turning their faces to a shiny brick-red. It would turn again to a pale leathery tan when they slowed down. But as yet they had no intentions of doing so.

Not until they reached that horizon, unmoving now, solid earth beneath their horses' feet, cropped grass bleached yellow where the sun beat on to it, did they give themselves and their mounts a breather. They looked down into a lush valley, a cluster of ranch buildings, the spreading tentacles and squares of corrals and fences, a thin, tortuous creek running like a silver snake. Behind them were herds of cattle in the distance.

'There it is,' snarled Kramer. 'The pigs'-wallow.'

'Whether or not, it's kinda beautiful,' said the blocky Olly.

'I'd like tuh blow it tuh Kingdom Come,' said Kramer. He kneed his horse, gently easing him down the slope. 'Wal, maybe we'll get tuh do jest that.'

'Wouldn't it be mebbe better tuh sort of creep up on 'em?' said Jim McDougal. 'I mean – if Lye Spar is—'

'What's the matter with yuh – yaller?'

'Yuh know I ain't, Lafe,' said McDougal hotly.

'Come on then. There won't be many there this time o' day, anyway. Most've 'em'll be out ridin'. If Spar is there now's our chance to get him.'

McDougal shrugged his shoulders and looked at Olly. Olly grinned at him. It didn't do no good to argue with Lafe when he was in a mood like this. All they could do was ride right along with him and watch out for him in his recklessness, so that he didn't get his head blown off.

Their horses' hooves thudded on hard-hammered sod as they reached level ground once more. Before them was an archway made from three stout tree trunks with the bark peeled from them. The crossbar one had been sawn flat at the front and a board nailed across it. On this, in freshly painted black letters, was inscribed: 'THE CROSS M RANCH.'

The three horsemen rode slowly beneath the archway, between green-painted wicket-fences and past the first empty corral.

'Fancy railings,' said Kramer scornfully. 'Dude ranch.'

He didn't miss much, but his eyes looked straight in front of him from beneath the wide brim of his sweat-stained Stetson. The other two were just as alert; their whole bearing denoted a subtle strain, nerves on hair-triggers. The three walking horses were neck and neck now, but a space between them so that they filled the drive. Olly Masters at one fence, Jim McDougal the other, Kramer in the middle. They held the reins loosely, their hands never far away from the guns on their thighs.

As they passed a large feed-barn, two men came around

a corner. They halted uncertainly at the sight of the newcomers. They looked surprised.

'Howdy,' said Kramer.

'Howdy,' they chorused rather weakly.

'We're kinda surprised tuh see you hyar, Kramer,' said one, a gangling beanpole whose gun sagged almost to his knees.

'We gotta little business with Lye Spar,' said Kramer. 'Have you seen him around?'

'Yeah, I thought I saw him ride in 'bout twenty minutes ago.'

His companion – another hard case – did not speak, but watched the three horsemen, with beady black eyes. His manner was markedly hostile. He looked like a gunny, too. His hardware was double and well forward for a quick draw.

Kramer said: 'Mebbe you boys'll turn around an' sort of go forward to announce us. Tell Spar to get the red carpet out. We want a big pow-wow with him.'

'Wal, we had got business,' said the beanpole uncertainty. 'But if you've come peaceful-like—' Evidently he hadn't heard of the furore in Georgetown.

His companion suddenly spoke – the first time since his grunted 'howdy' in the beginning. His voice was like gravel, his tones markedly aggressive. 'Have yuh ever known Trouble J bozoes come here in peace? They're up tuh no good 'cos the boss ain't here.'

Kramer said: 'I don't like your gab, fellah – I don't like your face, either.' He kneed his horse forward suddenly. The hard case backed, looking up into the saturnine face above him. His hands were claws but, wisely, he held them rigid. He tried to swing past but found his way barred once more as Kramer outmanoeuvred him.

'Say,' said the beanpole. He looked up at McDougal and Masters as their horses edged nearer to him. 'Look, fellahs—' He began to back beside his fuming companion.

'A fine welcome we get,' said Kramer. 'Turn around, both of yuh. An' keep walkin'.'

'I don't know what your game is,' snarled the smaller man. 'But it ain't—'

'Do as I say,' snarled Kramer, interrupting him. 'An' if you're thinkin' of tryin' any fast moves, don't! Right now you're too healthy. Do as you're told an' stay that way.'

'You talk too much,' retorted the other, but he turned.

The beanpole was already on his way. His plaintive tones floated back:

'This ain't right, fellahs.'

'Keep movin',' said Kramer. He didn't trust the skinny galoot. His meekness seemed to be a mite overdone.

Merv Judson's men were hand-picked. Every single one of them was a hard case. They needed watching all the time. Kramer figured these two were no exception to the rule.

'Hold your hands out at the sides where we can see 'em,' he rapped. 'Away from them guns. That's better. Act natural – keep healthy.'

'You're still talking too much,' said the smaller of the two men.

'Cut the lip,' snarled Kramer. 'Keep goin' steadily. Turn here.'

They were in sight of the ranch-house proper now. The three horsemen braced themselves. They were mighty fine targets if anybody up at the house there decided to take pot-shots at them.

Lafe Kramer slid from the saddle first, keeping a wary, eye on the two bobcats in front. McDougal and Masters followed suit. To the right of them, at an outbuilding that looked like a cook-house, a man appeared. He cast a cursory glance in the direction of the men and then disappeared again. The empty yard was bathed in glaring sunshine. The five humans were naked targets beneath it. In a patch of shade beneath an old tree an old dog lay sleeping.

'Where might Lye Spar be?' said Kramer.

'He might be in the bunk-house,' replied the beanpole, and changed his direction obligingly.

They approached the wide door of the long, low bunk-house with its four dusty windows. At right-angles to it was a small stable – shady, smelling of fodder and horseflesh. The hooves of the three strange horses made shuffling sounds in the dust; the footsteps of the men were muffled so as to be almost inaudible. The ceaseless hum of a myriad of tiny insects only seemed to intensify the quiet and the heat. Then the silence was shattered to a thousand pulsating fragments as a gun boomed. Smoke drifted from the dusk of the stables and Kramer's hat flew from his head.

He whirled, then froze. 'The next one'll be in your head,' said the man who came from the stables. He had a Colt in either hand. Behind him were two more gunnies, both armed to their eye-teeth.

'Up with your mitts,' said the first one.

Menaced by six guns, the three pardners could do nothing else but comply with this brusque command.

The bunk-house door opened and Lye Spar came out.

'Mawnin', boys,' he said. 'I saw yuh comin'. How do you like my little reception committee?'

'It stinks!' said Olly Masters.

'You're wanted for the murder of Bill Carter,' said Kramer. 'This little circus ain't gonna help yuh at all.'

'You sound like a tinpot lawman,' said Spar. 'Since when?'

Kramer didn't answer this one. He was watching the whiplike little gunman as if he'd like to sink his teeth into him.

'Murder's a nasty word,' said Spar with affected pomposity. 'An' since yuh didn't see the alleged murder how come you can shoot off your mouth about it? Who sent you here? Don't tell me. I know. You came here all on your own sayso, figuring to pay off some fancied scores. Your boss tried, an' he failed. I got plenty witnesses to say it was self-defence. You nor nobody else can pin a murder-rap on me.'

'I got plenty proof here tuh say yuh busted in on us, held up two o' the men, tried force to get me away an' avenge your boss. If you bat your eyelashes the boys'll let you have it.'

'Got it all figured out, haven't you?' said Kramer. 'Wal, go ahead—'

Spar laughed harshly. 'You're beggin' for it,' he said. 'Take their guns off them, boys.'

The beanpole, whose manner had undergone a change, moved forward with his beady-eyed pardner. One of the stable-skulking gunnies joined them.

'Gangin' up on us,' said Kramer.

'Yeah,' said McDougal. 'One man each: quite an honour.' He exchanged a swift glance with Masters.

The blocky man suddenly lowered his head and charged. He hit his beady-eyed contemporary full in the midriff. At the same time Kramer and McDougal moved, both getting their captors between them and the men with the guns.

The beanpole reached for his iron. Kramer moved in swiftly, driving a short-arm jab beneath the heart. The beanpole's fists came up to protect himself, but not before Kramer had rattled his teeth with a follow-up blow to the side of the jaw which made him totter.

Kramer heard Lye Spar give a sharp command, and out of the tail of his eye he saw the other men advancing, their guns clubbed.

The blond Jim McDougal's opponent was big and slow-moving. He never had a chance. He went down before a flurry of blows. The gun he drew was wrenched from his hand and sent spinning in the dust. McDougal dragged him to his feet by the sagging breast of his shirt and battered at him with a bony, rock-hard fist. Then a gun-barrel narrowly missed the lean man's ear, crashed with sickening force on his shoulder, driving him to his knees.

In the bunk-house doorway Spar stood and grinned. Things were working out fine. These three Trouble J boys would get a lesson they wouldn't forget in a hurry. However, he kept his hands on the butt of his guns, just in case.

Trying to make up for lost time, the big, slow man kicked at McDougal's face. He missed, but the other man's gun descended again. He began to pistol-whip the staggering McDougal with brutal finesse.

Meanwhile, the blocky Masters was wrestling with the beady-eyed hard case. They were squirming and twisting in the dust, locked together like a couple of grizzly-bears, so that any pistol-swinging galoot could not figure which was who. Consequently, Kramer got the attention of the other hard case and tackled both of them – one man swinging a gun-barrel, trying to get in a good crack and quieten this big fellah down a mite.

But Kramer was as slippery as a fistful of axle-grease. He got under the man's gun arm, sank a punch to his middle, drove another one to the lowering face. The man gulped and groaned as he buckled up. Kramer turned to meet a fresh onslaught of the beanpole. A haymaker caught him high up, on the head, knocking him sprawling, his brain giddy. It was only instinct that made him roll to one side as his attacker swung a heavy boot. Kramer grabbed the hovering leg. Caught off balance, the other's long length hit the dust with terrific force.

The burly gun-swinger was rising again. Too late, Kramer saw him and turned, crouching. The gun-barrel descended. He tried to dodge. The sharp steel tore the skin at his neck, bringing searing pain. It rose and fell again.

As Kramer teetered drunkenly, the beanpole rose again and began to beat at him with his fists.

The three men were outnumbered; and pitted against them were foes who used cold steel instead of bare fists.

Only Masters was really holding his own now. He rose, leaving his man squirming on all fours. Then, as his opponent rose, the blocky cowboy hit him with terrible force flush in the face. The man's heels kicked up miniature dust clouds, the back of his head almost dug a hole in the ground; he lay still.

Shaking his head like an enraged bull, Masters looked around him. Then he charged to the aid of McDougal, who was on his knees and being beaten into insensibility by two men.

It was then that Lye Spar left the comforting shade of his doorway and, gun in hand, joined the fray. Masters did not see him coming and was taken by surprise by a blow at his ear that made him see fireworks in the blackness and stagger like a drunkard. Spar hit him again and again; then, as he fell, began to put the boot to him.

Then he bawled: 'All right! That's enough! Have yuh got their guns?'

His plug-uglies came away from their battered victims. Each of them had a gun in each hand.

One by one, the three Trouble J men staggered to their feet. All the fight beaten out of them, they were in a sorry state; but, if the flesh was weak, the spirit was still willing; each of them watched their captors with blazing, hate-filled eyes – in McDougal's case, *one* hate-filled eye: the other was already a tight, purple mess.

'You're gettin' a chance this time,' said Spar. He was enjoying himself. 'Next time you're found trespassing on Cross M property you'll be shot on sight.'

'You're very generous, Mister Spar,' panted Kramer. 'Particularly as I'm givin' yuh warning right now that I mean tuh kill yuh next time we meet.'

Spar grinned again. 'I'll be lookin' for yuh. Get on your hosses.'

The three men limped across to their mounts and climbed laboriously into the saddles.

'Get goin',' said Spar. 'Keep ridin' – an' don't come back.'

The three men shook the reins and urged their horses forward. As they took the trail out under the archway, they heard the raucous laughter of the Cross M men floating on the still air behind them.

Half a mile further on they met Sheriff Budd, Deputy Hank O'Toole, and young Frank Carter.

'What the purple blazes happened to you three?' said the sheriff.

The fuming men told him. The old lawman wasn't too sympathetic. 'I told yuh to hold your hosses,' he said. 'We're goin' in to pick up Spar now.'

'We'll come back with yuh,' said Kramer. His two pards backed him up in this.

But the sheriff was leary. 'Yuh can't go back in that condition. You oughta go on to town an' see the doc – all three of yuh.'

'We'll manage. Anyway, they took our guns. We want 'em back.'

'Wal, if you've made up your minds about it, I guess there's nothin' I kin do tuh stop yuh. But no funny business!' The old lawman urged his horse forward impatiently, passing the three men. They turned to follow.

Young Frank kneed his horse beside Kramer's.

'We wuz outnumbered, kid,' said the Trouble J foreman. 'How're you feelin'? That's a nasty bump you've got.'

'I feel all right. I've had it bathed.' The kid had forgotten about his wound. His voice was deep, trembling, as he said: 'We'll pay 'em back, won't we, Lafe?'

'You bet we will!' said the man grimly.

They breasted the top of the rise and looked down into the valley.

'Come on,' said Sheriff Budd.

The ranch buildings were silent as they approached them. The old hound-dog still slept in the shade.

Then a man who looked like a cook came out to them. 'Howdy, Sheriff. Can I help yuh?'

'Tell Lye Spar he's wanted.'

The man raised his eyebrows. 'All right.' He went. The quiet and the heat was oppressive.

'He's probably made a run for it,' said Kramer.

'He'd be a fool tuh do that,' said the sheriff. 'Particularly if – like Judson says – he's pleadin' self-defence.'

Kramer surreptitiously patted a little bulge in his shirt front. His eyes glowed strangely in his bruised and blood-ied face.

Lye Spar came out of the bunk-house, a gun dangling in his hand.

Kramer drew the small-calibre gun from his shirt. The sheriff turned his head and saw it. Even as Kramer fired the old lawman's fist was swinging.

Lye Spar staggered, the gun falling from his hand. He held himself up against the jamb of the bunk-house door.

Kramer's little revolver flew from his hand as the sher-iff's huge fist buffeted his shoulder. He swayed in the saddle.

'You fool! He wuz comin' out. He wuz givin' himself up!'

'He had a gun,' said Kramer.

Deputy O'Toole had dismounted and crossed to Spar. 'He's jest creased in the shoulder,' he said.

Spar glared at Kramer. 'You skunk! I'll get yuh for that.'

'I figured yuh wouldn't like it,' said the Trouble J man. A ghost of a smile crossed his grim, battered visage.

'Get your hoss, Spar,' said Sheriff Budd. 'You're coming with us.'

The cook came into view again. He had evidently been skulking and listening. 'I'll get it, Lye.'

The rest of the Cross M boys, if they hadn't already rode out on to the range, were evidently lying low. Maybe they weren't inclined to buck the law, anyway – not without Judson's orders. They didn't mean to stick their necks out for Lye Spar. Anyway, most probably the boss had something up his sleeve. Spar would be back before they could turn around.

The cook brought the little gunnie's horse. He mounted. The little cavalcade turned about and set off.

THREE

That night the sheriff's office was visited by Lawyer Herbert Markson. He was a stocky, tubby man with a beaming piggy face and little piggy eyes. His manner was brisk, but his conversation garbled and punctuated by a dry legal cough. He was pretty straight, as small-town Western lawyers went, but he liked money – and Mervyn Judson, his prospective client, had plenty.

Markson and the sheriff talked things over.

'It's a clear case of self-defence,' was the lawyer's conclusion. 'Whether the fight was forced on Bill Carter or not, we cannot prove. By all accounts, he was doing all the talking and threatening. Ahem. An' he drew first.'

'Law's law, Joe, you ought to know that. And – ahem – on the evidence you've got at present you can't hold either of these two men. You'll have to let them out on bail; then the coroner will have to decide whether they should stand trial or not. They won't run away. Judson's too smart for that – ahem – and Spar does what Judson tells him.'

'Who'll go bail for 'em?' said the sheriff.

'They'll get bail all right, you know that.'

'Yeah, I know that,' said Joe Budd. Then airily: 'By the way, now I come to think of it, Merv Judson did ask tuh see yuh. You can go through now. You got ten minutes.'

Markson snorted: 'That's very good of you, Joe. I wonder you remembered to tell me.'

'I like playin' it straight, Bart,' said the sheriff grimly. 'But I'd be glad to see them two snakes swingin' in the breeze – that's just what this town needs.'

'You shouldn't've said that, Joe, I might use it against you.'

'Use it an' be damned to yuh,' snarled the sheriff as Markson passed through the door into the cell-block. He got up and lumbered after him.

He drew his gun as he unlocked the cell that housed Judson and his side-kick.

'Thanks for nothin', Joe,' said Judson.

Spar merely scowled and spat. The sheriff locked the door behind the lawyer. 'Ten minutes, Bart,' he said.

As he returned to the office, Deputy O'Toole entered it from the street.

He said: 'There's a kind of an underground feud goin' on between Judson supporters and Carter ones. Nothin's happened yet, but it's in the air. I wouldn't be surprised—'

'It's a nasty business,' said old Joe. His broad, lined face wore a frown. 'Them two sidewinders wanted ol' Bill outa the way. He wuz the only one who really bucked Judson. On the other hand, nearly everybody who saw the ruckus reckined ol' Joe asked for it—'

'Judson's usual hangers-on,' interrupted the deputy.

'Who's gonna prove that?' The sheriff paused, then he continued in a level, unemotional voice: 'Bill Carter was one o' my oldest friends. I've known him since he was a younker. I courted a girl before he won her off me and made her his wife. She died givin' birth tuh Frank. It broke Bill's heart. He never really did get over it. For months afterwards he kept away from the town. I only saw him once or twice when I rode out tuh the ranch. He'd become a changed man – cantankerous, plumb hornery. But he wuz never bad; he'd never do anybody real harm if he could help it. He believed in law and order – he'd fought to maintain it in this territory. But he believed in his rights as well, and he was plenty willing to fight for 'em. Always ready for a fight, was Bill. He'd fought plenty to protect that pore crippled kid of his. An' he didn't want the kid to come up the hard way like he did. He wanted him to have the way left smooth for him when the old man died. I guess Bill wasn't blameless. Him an' Kramer an' them trouble-shooters o' theirs have sure raised Cain lately—' The old man's unemotional tones had taken on a tremor and he was panting a little as he finished. That was a pretty big speech for the usually taciturn old lawman.

'It's hell!' said O'Toole. 'I—' He broke off scowling as Lawyer Markson came in.

'Ten minutes, Joe,' said the little tubby man primly.

'It's white of yuh to be so punctual, Bart,' said the sheriff with a little sardonic smile.

The lawyer coughed. 'I'll be seeing you,' he said. The door closed behind him.

The old sheriff leaned back and put his feet up on the desk. O'Toole looked at him with astonishment.

Joe said: 'We'll await developments. Then I guess we'll ride out tuh the Trouble J.'

Light dawned on O'Toole's mild, bovine features. 'I get yuh,' he said. He took the boss at his word and squatted down on the couch.

The next time the sheriff looked at him his tousled head was sunk on his chest and he was fast asleep.

He awoke with a start when the door was rapped and old Joe boomed: 'Come in.'

O'Toole sat upright, his eyes popping: it wasn't often the loveliest lady of the town paid a visit to the sheriff's office.

She was a gorgeous blonde. She had big baby-blue eyes; a tip-tilted nose; ripe, red lips, and hellishly tantalizing dimples in her plump cheeks. She wore something perched precariously on her head that looked like a bundle of multicoloured feathers. Despite the heat, she wore a fur around her shoulders. 'Rabbit' was all the deputy could think of to describe it, but it certainly didn't look amiss. The rest of her ensemble was a bewildering whirl of silk and satin, beads and bows. It made O'Toole's head spin to look at her.

She swept into the little room like a ship in full sail.

'Mornin', Sheriff,' she said sweetly.

'Mornin', Miss Milly.'

'Mornin', Hank.'

'Mornin', Miss Milly,' articulated the deputy.

'Get the lady a chair, Hank,' said the sheriff.

'Yeah – yeah, sure!'

O'Toole grabbed a chair from against the wall and slammed it down in front the desk with a zeal that almost broke its legs off.

'Thank you, Hank.' The young lady sat down primly, arraying her skirts around her. Hank gulped as he was vouchsafed a glimpse of a pretty calf, then she looked at him speculatively, her cheeks dimpled, and he shuffled back to his seat on the couch.

'What can I do for yuh, Miss Milly?' said Joe Budd.

She quit dimpling and said briskly: 'I've come to bail out Merv an' Lye. How much yuh askin'?'

The sheriff's eyes sparkled beneath shaggy brows. His answer was just as brisk. 'How much d'yuh think they're worth?'

The girl was a mite taken aback, but she quickly recovered. 'Come now, Mr Budd, that's no answer. How much do I think they're worth?' She gave a little toss of her head.

'Not much maybe.'

'Doggone it!' was the unladylike rejoinder. 'I didn't say that!'

'Maybe they're safer in jail. Maybe it'd be better for everybody concerned – for the 'ull town maybe – if they stayed in jail a mite longer.'

'I know nothin' about that. Merv wants to get out. He knows you can't keep him. I'm here to get him out.'

'Do you want him out?'

'Yeah, I guess I do. How much?'

'You're mighty impatient, Miss Milly,' said the sheriff. He seemed to be reflecting deeply while the girl's face pinkened and O'Toole watched her with calf-like eyes.

'All right,' said the old man. 'Although I don't think they're worth much, I'll take a thousand apiece for 'em.'

'That ain't buttons,' said Milly. 'But I'll call your bluff.'

She turned away from the popping eyes of the deputy. Her skirts rustled. O'Toole had another heavenly glimpse of a shapely, silk-clad calf as she bent a little. Then she straightened up and tossed two bundles of notes on the desk.

'There's a thousand in each,' she said.

'Thank you, Miss Milly.' The sheriff gave the keys to O'Toole. 'Let 'em out,' he said.

A couple of seconds later the big deputy shepherded Judson and Spar into the office.

The former said: 'Thank you, my dear,' and gave his arm to the girl.

Spar said: 'I'd like my guns back, Sheriff.'

'Sure, Lye.' The old man tossed a loaded gunbelt on the desk. 'Be careful with 'em,' he said.

Spar scowled as he buckled them on. Then, without another word, he strode to the door and opened it for the other two.

'Thank you, Lye,' said Judson. Then he turned to the sheriff.

Budd beat him to the punch. 'For the time bein' you're free, Judson, but watch yourself an' don't go no further than the ranch, either of yuh.'

'We won't,' said Judson. 'We'll play along with yuh. But I ain't forgettin' the hand you dealt us. You're ridin' for a fall, Joe.'

'Is that a threat?'

'Not at all, Joe. Maybe it's a prophecy.'

With this last parting shot the saloon-man quit the office behind his aide-de-camp and with his fair companion on his arm. O'Toole watched her charming womanly sway and the swagger of the man as he clipped her arm close to his side, and he felt mighty het-up. Then the door closed behind them.

'Goddam that smarmy galoot,' burst out Hank. 'He gets in my craw.'

Carter's Trouble J was a sizeable spread, though only a third as large as the Cross M. There were only two of them in the territory: other smaller spreads had sold out to Judson years ago.

Everybody wondered what would happen now Bill was dead and the legal owner of the ranch was the cripple kid, Frank. Would he sell out? It was well that he had a hard-bitten hellion like Lafe Kramer to champion him. Although Lafe was a mite too hasty for the comfort of most folks.

Thoughts such as these ran through the heads of the sheriff and his deputy as they rode the trail to the Trouble J, but, taciturn men both, they did not voice them. They'd done enough talking between themselves for one day. Too much. And they both figured they'd have some real fancy spieling to do ere long.

Like the Cross M, the Trouble J ranch buildings lay in a hollow; but the same stream that was such an asset and a feature of the former's layout, was right on the edge of the Trouble J land. In fact, Judson had tried to claim that that part of the stream, too, was in Cross M land. Bones were broken in the ensuing dispute before it quietened down. But all these little items simmered beneath the surface.

As the sheriff and his deputy approached the Trouble J buildings, they could not but admit that they presented a much more neglected and poorer appearance than they used to. The cattle they had seen on the range, too, seemed a pretty poor lot. The lawmen were puzzled.

They saw one or two riders, who hailed them; but, as they dismounted before the sagging porch of the ranch-house, everything was silent.

Then young Frank suddenly appeared like a pale wraith in the shadows of the front door.

He held a shotgun awkwardly in the crook of his crip-pled arm, his other hand inside the wide, hooped trigger-guard. When he saw who the visitors were, he lowered the gun.

'Mornin',' he said. 'Light down, will yuh?'

'Mornin', Frank. How are yuh?'

'Oh, fine.' The younker's voice held a strong note of bitterness.

He seemed suddenly old beyond his years. The sheriff hadn't taken a lot of notice of him before. He was just a kid – a pal of his own son, Oakland. And if the virile old lawman thought of him at all, it was with a vague pity and a memory of Bill Carter when young, his wife dead, and a crippled baby on his hands.

'Is Lafe around, Frank?'

The kid's blue eyes were hard. 'Nope. But he should be back soon for chow. Anyway, anything you gotta say you can tell me, yuh know, Mr Budd.'

Frank had always called him Mr Budd – never sheriff. But his voice now – the timbre of his words – had under-gone a subtle change. Old Joe realized with a little shock of surprise that Frank had already assumed the mantle of his father, the ownership of the Trouble J. He admired the kid as he stood there, a rather pitiful, crooked figure in the soft gloom of the shabby living-room.

The sheriff sat down on the lumpy sofa, his deputy beside him.

'Maybe you'd better take the weight off your feet,

Frank,' he said. 'I got an idea you ain't gonna like what I've gotta tell yuh.'

The boy's thin face did not change its sullen expression. The blue eyes, which seemed so enormous, showed little surprise. Somehow, the kid looked as if he was prepared for almost anything.

In terse, unemotional tones, Joe Budd told him of Judson and Spar's release on bail, of the defence they had built for themselves – a defence that would maybe get them off scot-free. The law could play some funny tricks.

Young Frank sprang to his feet. He was a kid again: a bitter, indignant, vengeful kid. Hate contorted his face and made his eyes glow largely, almost evilly.

'Law!' he spat. 'The law's no good tuh me. Judson robbed my pa fer years – then killed him. If the law cain't do anythin' about it, I will!'

'I know how yuh feel, son,' said the sheriff. 'But I don't want yuh to do anything you'll be sorry for. Frank – tell me all about the trouble between your dad an' Judson. All of it. Maybe it'll make you feel better—'

Young Frank slumped back into his chair. Although he hadn't got a lot of time for the law – his father had taught him that to get on in this world you had to do plenty fighting for yourself – he could not mistrust this hard-bitten old-timer who was the father of his best friend.

His passion was spent, but his voice was thick with bitterness again when he said:

'Judson was gonna turn us out. Turn us off the Trouble J altogether—'

'What?' said the sheriff. He sounded as if he could not believe his ears. His hard, lined face crumbled in surprise.

It was then that the cat-footed trouble-shooter, Lafe Kramer entered the room.

'Thet's quite true, sheriff,' he said.

'I don't get it!' said Joe Budd. 'Judson turn you off the

Trouble J! How could he? Ol' Bill never said anything to me about it—'

Kramer perched himself on the edge of the table.

'Ef you'll all set back an' listen,' he said, 'I'll tell yuh the 'ull story, right from the beginning.'

'All right,' said the sheriff testily, his usual patience deserting him. 'Let's hear it – shoot!'

'Wal, you all remember Merv Judson comin' here. 'Twas about seven years ago. He had money to burn. He wuz everybody's friend. Most folks liked him – he didn't begin to show the cloven hoof until a couple of years or more later—'

'Keep tuh the facts, Lafe.'

FOUR

'All right, sheriff.' The big cowboy hitched himself to a more comfortable position on the table.

'As you know, until Judson built the Cross M, this place was the biggest spread in the territory. But one thing you didn't know – probably didn't notice – was that it was just after Judson an' Spar an' one or two more of thet bunch arrived that Bill Carter began to have his big run of bad luck. Judson didn't have a ranch then, he was busy in town with the Curly Cat, and mighty popular he was, too. It was the first time Georgetown had had a real honky-tonk run on Eastern lines. An' Mr Judson was mighty generous; he had seemingly endless supplies of money, an' he lent it out right and left. He was pally with everybody – even Bill Carter, who hadn't much time for the townsfolk as a rule.

'Wal, it wasn't until Judson had been here a coupla years that he decided tuh buy himself a strip of land an' build a ranch. There wasn't much land in the territory, what with all the small spreads all around. Right away Judson started tuh buy these people out. He wuz purty generous, he offered fair prices; he succeeded in beating down those who wouldn't play ball. Purty soon he owned all the land hereabouts, except the Trouble J Range. He asked the boss tuh sell. O' course, ol' Bill refused. I was with him at the time. Judson jest laughed – he said he hadn't expected tuh get the Trouble J, anyway; he only asked as a matter of form, an' he didn't see any reason why him an' Bill Carter shouldn't be real good neighbours – an' maybe Bill, being an old hand, would be able to teach him a few things about the ranchin' business. I tell yuh, he wuz real smooth an' pally, he almost took me in, an' I'm a naturally suspicious cuss. When I mentioned that Judson seemed a mite *too* smooth, Bill said I wuz talkin' through my hat, maybe I wuz jealous or some-thin'. After that I kept my trap shut. I guess the ol'-timer was gettin' tired of his one-man 'no-talk' campaign against the townsfolk. Judson brought new interest to his life, made him forget his troubles, played up to him. He even consulted him about the building of the ranch, how tuh run things, an' all. But he didn't seem tuh change Bill's luck none. Accidents kept happening – that bunch of border thieves everybody wuz talkin' about kept peckin' at our herd an' vanishing intuh thin air. Leastways, everybody blamed thet bunch.' Kramer paused and looked quizzically at the sheriff.

The old-timer winced: those cow-thieves were a sore point with him. He said: 'They sure seemed tuh vanish intuh thin air.'

'Maybe the reason they vanished so quickly is because they came from right here in the territory. The few people who saw them an' lived tuh tell about it said they all wore masks. Rustlers who come from far afield don't usually bother to cover themselves up thetaway. They know it's little likely that anybody'd recognize 'em, anyway. But a man who really wants to keep his identity secret—'

'You're jest surmising,' broke in the cautious old-timer.

'All right. We'll talk about that later. I'm wandering away from my main talk.' Kramer cleared his throat. 'The rustlers started pickin' at the Cross M herds as soon as Judson moved 'em in—'

'That's what I wuz gonna say. He lost stock, too.'

'Yeah, but always a damsight less than the Trouble J.'

'Maybe because he'd got a bigger force of night-riders.'

'We won't argue about that now,' said Kramer. 'The fact

remained that the Trouble J was goin' on the rocks – an' ol' Bill was worryin' himself sick. Judson offered to buy the ranch again – Bill wasn't as young as he useter be, wouldn't he like to settle down in a little house some place with young Frank? Judson promised to find work for me an' the rest of the men.' Kramer laughed harshly. 'As if I'd work for that buzzard! But Bill was adamant: he would not sell. He'd keep on struggling along. I guess it was more for Frank's sake as anythin'. Bill had ambitions of his son bein' a mighty big ranch-owner some day—'

'He did that,' said Frank softly, almost to himself. Kramer stopped for a moment; then, when he realized the youth had no more to say, he continued with his tale. 'Then Judson made him another proposition – uh – as a friend as well as a business man. He wouldn't presume to offer Bill charity, but he would lend him enough money to get on his feet with – just as a matter of business. Bill tumbled for it. He didn't even consult me, like he used to over most things. He took Judson's money, and mortgaged all his holdings to him—'

'I never knew anythin' about that,' said Sheriff Budd.

'At first, only *I* knew,' said Kramer. 'I didn't like it, but I couldn't do anything about it; Bill had signed papers an', everythin'. I guess if I'd've known in time I still couldn't't've done anythin' – you know what the boss was once he got the bit between his teeth.'

'I didn't know nothin' about it till years later,' said young Frank. Then he fell silent again.

Kramer continued:

'With the money, the boss paid off his debts, got things ship-shape, bought more cattle. For a bit, everythin' seemed rosy – even them pesky rustlers left us alone for a bit. But maybe that was because Bill could afford to hire more hands and we had a stronger force o' night-riders. That wuz about the time those owl-hooters vanished for a mite, Sheriff, yuh remember?'

'Yeah, I remember.'

'Wal, as I said, everything seemed rosy. Then Judson began to show the cloven hoof. It showed in town first when he began to foreclose on some o' the property that he held mortgages on there – turned the people out on their ears. It was a big surprise to everybody. Judson an' his boys must've bin splittin' their sides laughin'—'

'Yeah, it was a raw deal, all right,' said Joe Budd. 'It surprised me. An' I couldn't do a thing. Law's law, an' Judson made plenty sure he kept jest within it.'

'Yeah, an' after he'd cleaned the town out an' owned almost everything in it, he began to crowd us. He never came near us himself now – if he sent a message, it wuz alus through a bunch o' gunnies. We came mighty close to havin' a few killings. He began to press for his money. Bill paid some back – figuring to keep his mouth shut. But it soon became evident that it wasn't the money Judson wanted. He wanted the Trouble J land. He wanted to be the Grand Panjandrum of all this territory—'

'It's an old story,' said Joe Budd.

'I know,' said Kramer. 'An' it stinks more each time it's told. In many ways Bill Carter wuz a simple man; he was cantankerous, kind of hornery, but he was trustin'. An', like most trustin' people, when he discovered he'd bin tricked he started tuh raise Cain. An' all the time Judson was pickin' at him an' makin' things worse. There wuz that squabble over the water rights—'

'Yeah, I thought I wuz gonna have a range war on my hands,' said the sheriff. 'But Judson seemed to cool down purty quick.'

'Yeah, because it didn't suit his book to have open warfare,' said Kramer. 'He wanted to make it seem as if Bill was tuh blame fer all the trouble.'

'He almost had *me* believin' that for a time,' said the sheriff sadly. 'Why didn't Bill tell me? We wuz pards for a good many years—'

'You wuz his best friend,' said Kramer. 'He knew you'd do all you could if you knew. He thought that in bein' his friend you'd forget you were also a lawman. He didn't want you to stick your neck out. I guess he wuz kinda proud, too. He wuz allus the sort who wanted to fight the world all on his lonesome.'

'Yeah,' said Joe Budd. 'He was. The ol' buzzard.' Then in a whisper: 'God rest his soul.'

Kramer said: 'The other day Judson gave him seven days' notice. If he didn't pay up in that time he'd be turned out on his ear. Judson knew that Bill couldn't possibly get the money. When Bill went to the Curly Cat that mornin' it wuz to ask for more time. I guess it stuck in his craw, havin' to ask Judson like that. It was Frank he wuz thinkin' of all the time – that dream he had for Frank. He wouldn't let me go in with him tuh see Judson. I had to hang around town, an' I wuz scared all the time. I knew Bill wouldn't get a break. I guess Judson got tired o' playin' around, and when Bill lost his temper saw his chance to finish things once an' for all. I guess he figured his gunnies could handle the rest of us.'

That last sentence had an ominous echo as Kramer slid from the table.

'God, I could do with a drink after all that,' he said. 'How about it, Frank?'

The boy started. His eyes were dark.

'Yeah, sure,' he said. He crossed to a cupboard, opened it and produced a bottle of whiskey and four glasses. He poured a couple of fingers in each glass.

The sheriff said: 'I didn't think you drank, Frank.'

The youth did not seem to hear him. He tipped the red-eye back as if it were warm water. And Joe Budd had that uncomfortable, almost sad feeling again. Here was no boy, but an old, old man, with a heart black and full of hate. Hate in the strange, glowing eyes, the cruel twist of the crippled arm, the yellow hand with two claws like a bird of prey.

Joe shook his head and downed his whiskey. He was getting fanciful in his old age.

Nevertheless, he was not surprised at the ominous tones of the youth's voice as he said, as if voicing the tail-end of bitter thoughts: 'An' Judson thinks he's gonna turn us out in a coupla days or so. I guess he's got a surprise comin' to him, ain't he, Lafe?'

'I guess he has,' said Lafe with no trace of emotion at all.

'Don't be too hasty, boys,' said the sheriff. 'Maybe Judson won't feel so smart in a coupla days' time. I'll be pushin' for a trial of both him an' Spar. Wait till after the inquest, boys.' His hard face was furrowed with worry, his harsh voice almost pleading.

'We'll do that, Sheriff,' said Kramer. 'You've bin mighty decent. That's the least we can do.'

But as he left the ranch-house, Joe Budd was little reassured. For the first time in his life, he was scared. He felt old and powerless. He feared what the verdict would be at the inquest on Bill Carter.

Judson had a saloonful of witnesses; the coroner gave a verdict of self-defence, censured the two men verbally, but otherwise let them go entirely free. That young Frank Carter suddenly drew a gun and, if it wasn't for the timely intervention of Hank O'Toole, would have probably shot somebody, did not help matters, and anything Sheriff Budd might've done to foil Judson's schemes had to go by the board. Helped by the rest of the Trouble J men, Frank got away. The law did not think it worth while to chase him, although Lawyer Markson was heard to remark: 'You'll have to keep an eye on that young man, Joe. He's dangerous.'

That night three men and a boy stood at a grave on the hillside behind the Trouble J. They were Frank Carter, Lafe Kramer, Olly Masters, and Jim McDougal. Frank had elected to dispense with the services of a 'fancy preacher,' so Kramer said the short burial service; then afterwards, while the youth watched, the three men filled in the grave.

They did not hear the youth's whispered words: 'Even if Judson does get this land, Pa will still be there. An' if any of 'em ever touches his grave, I'll find him an' kill him, by heaven, I will.' Strange words for a seventeen-year-old boy; but, if the previous few days had made a man of him, this last night had tempered the steel and made it hard, unbending. There was no grief in the young man's heart now. Only bitterness and hatred and a cold resolve.

Kramer and his two side-kicks finished their task and placed the wooden headboard, on which names and dates had been inscribed with a hot iron, at the head of the mound. They arose, dusting down their chaps.

'Come on Frank,' said Kramer.

'Leave me a bit,' said the young man.

'All right.' Softly, they left him.

Frank went and knelt beside the grave. His head was bent. For a few minutes he was like a quiet image; then suddenly he spoke. His voice was harsh in the stillness.

'I'll get them, Pa. I swear it. I'll pay them back.'

He rose and stood erect. His head was high, but his withered arm made a pitiful silhouette. He turned suddenly away from the grave and stole softly into the blackness.

When he reached the stables he could hear the boys talking quietly in the bunk-house next door. He saddled his paint pony. Then he went into the deep gloom at the back of the stables. When he returned he carried a sawn-off shotgun. Awkwardly, he shoved this into the long leather boot beside the saddle.

He led the beast out; then, when he considered he was out of earshot of the bunk-house, he mounted and began to ride.

Inside the long, lantern-lit cabin, Olly Masters said: 'Hark! I thought I heard a horse.'

They listened. Lafe Kramer said: 'I don't hear nothin'.'

Jim McDougal said: 'Maybe it wuz one o' the boys.'

Masters crossed to the door and opened it. With native caution, he already had his hand on the butt of his gun. Kramer came up behind him and said: 'I wonder if it wuz young Frank. He's bin out there a while. He ought to be comin' in now. I feel kinda worried. I'm goin' up there.'

He strode past Masters. McDougal called: 'Watch yourself, Lafe, it might be Judson's men up tuh some tricks.' He joined the dark, blocky man in the doorway. The lamplight gleamed on his own blond locks.

'We're mighty conspicuous here,' said Masters.

'Yeah, let's get outside. Shut the door.'

They stood in the darkness, listening, straining their eyes, waiting. It seemed ages before Kramer returned. He was running.

'He's not there,' he panted. He ran on to the stables. They heard him blundering about in the darkness. Then he called: 'Come on. We gotta ride. The kid's paint ain't here.'

They joined him. As they led their horses out, Kramer said: 'Goddam it! We never ought to've left him. It's purty certain where he must've gone. The crazy young cuss.'

Meanwhile, Frank Carter was riding hard. His body jerked in the saddle, but his mind was washed of emotion, his brain ice-cold. When he heard the sound of cattle, and knowing that there would probably be night-riders near, he made a detour.

When he reached the hill above the Cross M Ranch he made another wide detour, not beginning to descend the slope until he was sure he was right behind the layout. He took it easy, gentling the frisky little paint with his good hand. He knew he was in danger. Approaching stealthily like this, if he was spotted, he was liable to be shot at; but he had no thoughts of turning back.

The beast's hooves struck level ground, hard sod. Frank halted him. He listened. The breeze soughed, the grass swished as the wind whipped it gently. In the distance came the mournful bellowing of cattle.

The backs of the Cross M ranch buildings were all in darkness, except for one faint glimmer. Frank figured that would be the cook-house. And the ranch-house was over to the left there.

He dismounted and began to walk his pony nearer. He left him in a clump of bare trees about fifty yards behind the ranch-house. He knew the faithful beast would stay there until he returned. He took the shotgun from the boot and cradled it in his crooked arm, holding it steady with his other hand, his finger close to the trigger. He would never be a fast-drawing gunman; but, at close range, a sawn-off shotgun was even more deadly. And the closer he got to the men he sought, the better he'd like it. He couldn't afford any slip-ups – he had to do what he'd got to do. And after that? He hadn't thought about it – he didn't care a whole lot what happened after that.

He ran lightly up the step on to the back porch. He pressed himself against the log wall beside the back door and listened. The silence was as absolute as a Western night can be. Frank would have been better pleased could he have heard a sound or two. He began to have a sense of failure. He shook it off impatiently, and tried the back door. It was locked.

He cursed softly between his teeth and slid along to the nearest window. The lower sash was up a little. He put his good hand to it. With a faint squeak, it rose. He climbed through and stood in the blackness listening once more.

There was still no sound except that, in here, the sound of the wind outside seemed somehow louder. He stood stock still, patiently waiting until his eyes were more accustomed to this deeper darkness.

He realized he was in a kitchen. There was another door right opposite him. He crossed to it, opened it gently, expecting to see a light somewhere beyond. Then he opened it wide – all was blackness again.

He halted once more. He was in the living-room now. Surely if there was anyone in the house at all he should be aware of it now. Probably Judson was in town. He was a bachelor, and whoever he kept here to do for him was probably out, too, or in the bunk-house.

For the first time, Frank cursed himself for being a crazy young fool. However, he passed through the living-room into the hall and softly climbed the stairs. But up there, too, he drew another blank.

He retraced his steps, leaving the house the same way he had entered. But still he was not satisfied. He began to prowl around the other buildings, hate for the Cross M and everything connected with it growing in his heart all the time, the double-barrelled shotgun held ready in his arm, ready to disgorge half its contents at a pressure of his finger.

He heard horses champing in a feed-stable, and slunk into there. Maybe he could raise some kind of hell, anyway. He felt for matches, and cursed. He had not brought any with him.

But he wasn't helpless! He began to untether the horses in their stalls. Again he cursed his disability; his left hand had to do all the work. He was fumbling when the rays of a lantern lit up the door of the stables. Frank dropped to one knee in the shadow of the stall.

A big man entered, a hurricane-lantern swinging in his hand. He peered about him: he could've sworn he'd heard somebody in here.

'Anybody there?' he said.

Frank held his breath and kept perfectly still. The big man shrugged his shoulders and came further into the stable – making straight for the stall where the younker crouched. Frank thought fast. He could not risk being seen. He had to stop this big fellah.

He pitched his voice low, and said: 'All right, I've got yuh covered. Put the lamp on the floor an' raise your hands.'

The big man stopped in his tracks, his mouth gaping, his eyes popping.

'Yeah,' he said. He bent, then he went for his gun.

Frank pressed the trigger of the sawn-off shotgun. It boomed; placed as he was, the recoil almost knocked him flat on his back.

The big man keeled over. The lamp crashed from his hand, rolling as the glass shattered. The flames licked at the straw that carpeted the floor.

Frank didn't await developments. He ran from the place and around the corner. His paint was waiting patiently; the younker forked him and set off at a mad gallop. He felt a wild exultation. At least he had done something! Whether the big man was alive or dead, he did not know. He certainly did not care. If the man wasn't already dead he was in danger of being roasted alive. Frank found himself chuckling at the thought, and felt no surprise at his own callousness. He realized that he had never been sensitive to the sufferings of others. He knew he would glory in the suffering of any of the Cross M people. He was pledged to destroy them all – or die in the attempt.

He began to make a detour. His brain was still ice-cold. He knew he would get away.

FIVE

The three riders heard the muffled thud of the shotgun.

'I hope that's not what I think it is,' panted Lafe Kramer. 'If the crazy young cuss's killed anybody, I guess we cain't do nothin' else but try tuh get him away all in one piece. I hope tuh gosh he ain't bin recognized, or we *are* sunk!'

They reined in at the crest of the rise. Down below, lights were beginning to flash. There was a glow at the end of the sprawling row of buildings. As the horsemen watched, the glow spouted tongues of flame.

'Looks like Frank's set the place on fire,' said Olly Masters, half-jocularly.

Jim McDougal said: 'Listen! There's hosses comin'.'

They halted. 'One hoss,' said Kramer. Then the rider was upon them. A weapon glinted in his hand.

'Frank!' bawled Kramer.

'Get goin',' yelled the younker. 'Ride like hell!'

They turned their rearing horses and bunched themselves around him. They galloped. 'Did yuh get spotted?' yelled Kramer. The wind whipped his words away, but Frank heard him. 'Nope. I shot a guy. He didn't see me. He's maybe dead an' cain't talk, anyway. If we keep goin' they won't know which way I came, either. I left by the back way. We've got a good start. They'll be too busy fightin' the fire tuh do a lot of chasin' yet awhile—'

'Good fer you, kid!' yelled Kramer.

When they were nearing their own spread they halted on the wind-blown mesa and listened. There were no sounds of pursuit.

When they entered the stables, Kramer said: 'Give the hosses a good rub an' bed 'em down. Who's tuh tell they've bin ridden to-night? Then we'll bunk down ourselves; but keep your guns handy, in case them Cross M skunks come investigating.'

'Don't we allus keep our guns handy?' said Jim McDougal sardonically.

A few minutes later they were tucked between the sheets in the empty bunk-house. Three of the men had left with their pay; two were night-riding. The other three who made up the eight of the remaining personnel of the small ranch had the night off and had gone into town. Things were sort of hanging fire – Frank didn't know whether he'd have a ranch on which to employ any men within the next few days.

When hoofbeats did clatter outside, the three wide-awake men feared the worst and sprang to their feet with guns at the ready.

'Don't sound like many of 'em,' said the phlegmatic McDougal. 'Only two maybe. That's queer.'

They heard the riders rein in. Then a voice bawled 'Frank! Lafe!'

'It's the sheriff,' said Kramer.

'He promised tuh come earlier,' said Frank. 'I didn't expect him at all tonight – not this late. Sounds like something's eating him.'

In his new pose of leader, he was first at the door. He swung it open and was almost knocked over by the huge bulk of the sheriff.

'Sorry tuh bust in so late. I got some news for yuh – an' I want to apologize for not comin' earlier.' He had promised to be present at the burial of his old pardner, Bill.

Hank O'Toole followed the sheriff into the bunk-
house. Kramer lit the lamp.

The two lawmen sat themselves on empty bunks.

'Let's hear the news,' said Kramer. The four Trouble J
boys were keyed-up. Surely the sheriff hadn't already
heard of the Cross M ruckus?

The sheriff lit a quirly. His voice was pleasantly conver-
sational when he said: 'Three of your boys've bin raising
hell in town. I got two of 'em in jail. The other's at Doc's
with a broken jaw—'

'Bennett, Dobson, an' Pretty,' said Kramer.

'Yeah. Pretty's the one wi' the broken jaw. One of
Judson's men is laid up with a slug in his guts. He may not
live. I've got four Judson men in jail, too—' The sheriff
looked at Frank. 'That's why I didn't come like I promised,
younker—'

'I understand, Mr Budd.'

Then Kramer spoke up, but softly: 'You're not suggest-
ing, are you, Sheriff, that we sent those three men tuh
town to start a ruckus?'

The old man shook his leonine head. 'No-o.'

'We knew they'd gone intuh town, that's all. Anyway,
what started the ruckus? Where did it happen?'

'In the Curly Cat. It seems that jest before closing time,
one o' Judson's men started makin' cracks about you boys.
Big Bill Pretty heard him – you know how Bill loves a fight
– wal, right away he started one. He threw the big-
mouthed *hombre* through the nearest window. He was set
upon right away by the Curly Cat's pet bouncers, an' naturally, Bennett an' Dobson went to his aid. That started a
first-class ruckus – you've still got plenty supporters in
town. Hank an' me an' a few of the more peaceable townsfolk had quite a task to quieten things down. As soon as I'd
got things ship-shape an' sworn in a few special depities to
guard the jail an' keep order, me an' Hank rode out
here—'

'Oh, my gosh!' burst out Olly Masters. 'We miss all the goddamed fun. Here's us bin poundin' our ears while all that's bin goin' on.'

The sheriff jerked up his head suddenly. 'Somebody's comin'.'

'Quite a bunch, too, by the sound of 'em,' said Kramer. 'I wonder who it can be?'

They weren't left long in doubt, for as the horses clattered to a mumbling stop, a stone crashed through the window and the harsh voice of Mervyn Judson, trembling now with passion, bawled: 'You'd better come outa there pronto, all of yuh, or we'll come in an' get yuh!'

Then the inevitable rasping tones of Lye Spar chimed in with: 'Or we'll burn the place over your heads like yuh tried tuh do to the Cross M.'

'What crazy foolishness is this?' said Sheriff Budd, gazing in bewilderment at the others.

In the shadow of a bunk, Frank Carter sat silent. McDougal and Masters reached for their guns and padded to positions, one each side of the door. Kramer buckled on his gunbelt. His eyes were glittering slits.

He said: 'I don't know what foolishness it is, but it's evidently dangerous to all of us. Them folks ain't fooling – they mean business.'

The sheriff raised his bull-like voice: 'Judson! This is Sheriff Budd. Whadyuh think you're playin' at?'

There were startled exclamations from outside, then Judson said: 'Come on out here, Joe, we got somethin' mighty interestin' tuh tell yuh.'

The sheriff crossed to the door and flung it open. The men inside the lamp-lit bunk-house grew tense. Joe Budd's huge shape almost blocked the doorway. In the shafts of light that escaped, Frank Carter could see the packed ranks of horsemen outside. He had a queer, hollow feeling in the pit of his stomach. His shotgun, cleaned and reloaded, was stashed away beneath the straw in the corner of the stables. He wished he had it with him right now.

The sheriff said: 'All right, Merv, what's bitin' yuh? Spill it!'

When he replied, the saloon-cum-ranch-owner's voice was controlled again.

'We know now what wuz the purpose behind the ruckus staged in the Curly Cat by them Trouble J gunnies. They wanted to keep as many of our people back there in town while their pards here sneaked up on the Cross M an' started a fire. They might've razed the place to the around if one o' my men hadn't spotted 'em an' give the alarm—'

'This man o' yourn. Is he sure it wuz Trouble J men he saw?'

'Yeah, he wuz sure all right.'

'Where is he?'

'He's daid. One o' them skunks filled him with buck-shot. But he talked before he died. He said it wuz Trouble J men all right. It's murder now as well as arson, Sheriff.'

Inside the bunk-house, a glance passed between Lafe, Kramer, and Frank Carter. The kid gave an almost imper-ceptible shake of his head: he was sure the big man in the Cross M feed-barn had not seen him.

Kramer took a chance. He joined Sheriff Budd in the doorway and, with passion that was not hard to simulate, bawled: 'You're tellin' a pack of made-up lies, Judson. We bin here all night. We wuz asleep when the sheriff called – he can vouch for that.'

The sheriff said: 'The place was in darkness. You suttinly seemed to—' The rest of his sentence was drowned by a howl from the mob outside, as they had their first look at Kramer. He was taking an awful chance standing there in the lamplight.

'Let them skunks come out an' take their medicine, Sheriff,' shouted Lye Spar. 'Your law's no good here.'

Joe Budd stepped out on to the hard ground. His huge

shadow spread and loomed as he stood, feet apart, his hands dangling near his guns.

'My law's good anywhere in this territory, Spar,' he snarled. 'You've bin flyin' mighty high lately – but mind you don't bump your haid. You don't think I'm gonna stand by an' see you do what you will with men who may be entirely innocent of what you accuse them.'

'You're on their side,' growled Spar. 'I'd like tuh know what you're doin' here, anyway. An' here's your depity, look – all pals together.'

A spate of laughter from the Cross M men greeted this sally as Hank O'Toole loomed to a position beside his boss. They looked a formidable pair.

'Let me take the little skunk apart, Joe,' said O'Toole. But Spar heard him. His voice was a hiss: 'I could fill you full o' lead.'

'I shouldn't try it,' rasped another voice, and Lafe Kramer joined the other two.

'I shouldn't at that,' boomed the sardonic voice of Olly Masters.

He stood at the open window of the bunk-house. There was a Colt in each of his hands. At the window the other side of the door was Jim McDougal. He, too, had each fist packed with a deadly smokepole.

Young Frank came through the door and joined Joe Budd, O'Toole, and Kramer outside. He held a Colt awkwardly in the left hand.

'Even the baby's come out tuh show us his toy,' jeered Spar. But his voice had an uneasy timbre.

The sheriff said: 'Any of you can draw – but a good many, of you – including the two boss-men – will be daid pigeons before you could do much blasting.' Whether the sheriff was pleased or otherwise about this sudden move on the part of the Trouble J men was not revealed in the level tones of his voice.

As the lawman spoke, Jim McDougal moved swiftly away

from the window. Then the bunk-house lamp went out. McDougal returned to his post, his guns, like his pard, Masters, now only small steel glints in the darkness.

The Cross M bluff had been called. It was a bluff that might mean the death of the lawmen and their friends. But they'd manage to take a whole lot of the Cross M with them to Kingdom Come.

At the thought of that, a cold sweat broke out on the broad forehead of Mervyn Judson. Bulked there on his horse, he felt a very vulnerable target. Those vague, tense shapes standing in front of and inside the bunk-house could do terrible things to him.

He didn't lack ruthless guts, but he wasn't that brave. He began to bluster.

'Sheriff Budd, I demand you arrest these men on a charge of arson an' murder.'

The sheriff said: 'Don't try tuh force my hand, Judson. Right now, I don't like your play. I'll do things my own way. Right now, I'd advise you an' your men tuh turn around an' go right back home.'

'What! No bedtime story?' said a voice at the back of the bunch. The snarl of Lye Spar cut them aside.

'Go back, the sheriff says! Go back with our tails between our legs. Let these fire-bugs an' back-shootin' friends of his go off scot-free—'

'You're askin' fer trouble, Spar,' warned the sheriff.

'Easy, Lye,' said Judson. He was diplomatic; but Spar, cur though he was, had more guts and recklessness than his boss. He ignored him.

'Ye-ah!' he bawled at the sheriff, and for the benefit of his followers: 'We oughta take these skunks out an' swing 'em from the nearest tree.'

Sheriff Budd said: 'The first step you make towards that design'll be your last on this earth, Spar.'

'I'll second that,' snarled Lafe Kramer.

Spar said: 'I cain't do much about an ol' man who hides

behind a tin badge. But you ain't wearin' no badge, Kramer. I'll take you on any time.' The little gunman was really playing up to his followers now.

Kramer called his bluff. His voice was ice-cold as he said: 'I'll take yuh up on that, Spar. I'll be ridin' into Georgetown at noon tomorrer. You'd better be waitin', unless you want to be labelled a yeller skunk for all time.'

The gauntlet had been slammed down now with a vengeance. The ensuing silence was like a sudden blanket, which seemed to muffle even the myriad sounds of the night. A cold, noiseless wind blew.

Spar's voice in the stillness was like the tolling of a cracked bell. He said: 'I'll be there.'

'You heard that, Sheriff,' said Kramer. 'A straight challenge, accepted. I ride intuh Georgetown alone tomorrow, an' if I don't get dry-gulched by some of his fancy friends, I'm gonna kill that skunk.'

'I heard it,' said the sheriff. 'I ain't committing myself right now; but I will say there'll be no dry-gulching in Georgetown while I'm there.'

'I don't want a lot of bloodshed,' said Judson pompously. 'I want justice. I cain't stay here argufyin' all night.' He was turning his horse when he shot home his last bolt – a flash of bravado to save his lost face. 'I'm warnin' you, Sheriff. I won't be bamboozled. If you want war, you can have it—'

'Goddam 'em,' said Joe Budd as the Cross M party rode away.

Then he turned to Kramer. His voice was toneless again as he said: 'Where are your hosses?'

'In the stables.'

'Let me see them.'

'You still think we might've done what Judson—'

'What I think or what I don't think has nothin' tuh do with it,' interruped the sheriff. 'I've gotta job tuh do. I'd like to see them horses.'

'All right.' Kramer led the way to the stables. Everybody followed him. He lit the hanging lantern in there.

The sheriff inspected the horses, running his hands over their glossy hides.

Then he snorted: 'Don't know what I expected tuh find.' He turned suddenly on Frank. 'Haven't I seen you with a shotgun, younker?'

'Yeah, maybe you have.'

'Where is it?'

'Wal, Pa useter bawl me out if he saw me with it, so I allus kept it hidden. I ain't dug it out since. Here it is.'

He crossed to the corner of the stables and pulled back the straw. The sheriff followed him and picked the weapon up.

'It's shined up mighty pretty.'

'Yeah, I allus keep it that way,' said the kid. 'I never know when I might need it.'

Watching him, his face blank, Lafe Kramer admired Frank's coolness. The cold-blooded young skunk – he shore was full of surprises since his dad died. The sheriff didn't seem to suspect anything at all – he seemed to be carrying out his investigations just as a matter of form. It was a shame to pull the wool over his eyes. He was a squareshooter. But Kramer knew what the old man would do – he'd feel himself compelled to do – if he knew the truth—

The sheriff sniffed at the double-barrels of the shotgun. All he could smell was oil.

He handed the gun to Frank. 'No need to hide it any more, is there?' he said drily. 'Like you say, you never know when you might need it.'

'Thanks, Mr Budd,' said the youth. He held the shotgun in his crooked arm and stroked the shiny barrel absently with his good hand.

The sheriff said: 'I want tuh see you boys in town tomorrow mornin'.'

'I ain't comin' in till noon,' said Kramer grimly.

Frank interposed: 'I kin tell you anythin' yuh wanta know, Mr Budd. I'll ride in first thing. Anyway, I'd like tuh see how Big Bill's busted jaw's gettin' on, an' how them boys in jail are faring. It's throwin' us mighty short-handed tomorrer.'

'That cain't be helped,' said the sheriff. 'Maybe I'll let 'em out tomorrow afternoon. I cain't hold 'em indefinitely, for somethin' almost everybody wuz tuh blame fer. I only hope that Judson man don't cash in his chips.'

All his listeners were very much aware that a hell of a lot might happen before tomorrow afternoon arrived.

Joe Budd turned to his deputy. 'Come on,' he said. 'Let's get goin'. We'll go an' see the damage at the Cross M first thing tomorrer. See you about ten, Frank?'

'Sure, Mr Budd.'

SIX

By eleven-thirty a.m. Frank had not returned from his visit to the sheriff, so Kramer got ready for his dramatic rendezvous in town. He had meant to wait for the younker, but more important was the fact that he mustn't keep Lye Spar waiting. He certainly didn't intend to. Maybe he'd meet Frank on the trail. He hoped to gosh the kid hadn't stayed in town to breed a misguided attempt at helping his friend – surely the sheriff would prevent him from sticking his neck out like that. Kramer was worried. Even if the odds were against him – and he mistrusted Spar and Judson's ability to play straight, he didn't want the kid to get mixed up in the ruckus. Masters and McDougal had wanted to come, but Kramer insisted on playing it alone. He knew that, despite his orders, they would light out after him as soon as he was out of sight. He had to admit that he might be mighty glad of their help before the day was out.

As he rode the trail he tried to wash his mind clear of thoughts, but the niggling anxiety for Frank – curse the crazy young coot, he was so unpredictable lately! – still remained in the back. That was bad. His brain must be ice-cold, his mind clear, if he wanted to make sure of a fast gun like Spar – and whatever little tricks he might have up his sleeve, too. Kramer was a very proficient gunman. He knew that the quickness of his hand and his eyes, and the coolness of his brain, were the only things that pulled him through. If he let any one of these qualities slack for one split second it might mean his finish.

If by worrying about the kid he impaired his own efficiency and got himself killed, he wouldn't be of much help to the kid, anyway. So to hell with him! And on to Lye Spar! It would give him great pleasure to shoot that little gunnie plumb between the eyes – like exterminating a diamond-back rattler.

The sun was reaching its zenith. Kramer blew out a gust of breath and mopped his streaming face with the tail of his bandanna. He was approaching the sandstone bluffs that were roughly half-way between the Trouble J Ranch and the town. He squinted into the sun-glare, spat drily, and thought of nothing else but getting to his destination.

He passed beside the bluffs and the shade was cool and peaceful. He hardly saw the wide loop that dropped over his head from above. Instinct made him reach for his guns. His hands were on the butts when the noose tightened around his wrists and he was powerless.

The next moment he seemed to be surrounded by masked men – dozens of them – although in reality there were only four or five. He kicked out as one of them advanced, and had the satisfaction of hearing the man grunt, of seeing him clutch at his middle, and double up. Then one of them clutched him the other side and dragged him from his horse.

He hit the ground with a thud that knocked all the breath out of him. A knee was ground into his chest. Two gleaming eyes looked down at him through the slits of a black mask that covered the rest of the face. A big hand clapped a damp cloth over his mouth. There was the terrible sickly sweet smell of chloroform. Kramer tried to fight, but his senses swam and groped in a pink haze that became purple, then there was utter blackness and oblivion.

The sun, like a globe of molten brass, seemed to revolve in the sky directly above Georgetown; and Frank Carter, crouching in the cover of a disused stable, watched it with awe and a feeling of frustration and disappointment. Surely it was noon? Maybe well past.

In the dusty shadows behind him, Frank's paint pony stood motionless. From where he crouched, Frank could see a sun-bathed stretch of Main Street and the doors of the Curly Cat. The street was deserted: the good people of Georgetown, in anticipation of fireworks, were holed-up. Frank figured there wasn't much danger of his being spotted.

Sheriff Budd had insisted that the youth get out of town pronto. Frank had ridden out in a cloud of dust, but once out of sight had made a detour and ridden in quietly along the 'backs' of Main Street. He had entered the disused stables through a gaping hole in the back. He knew the place well, it had been a favourite playground of 'Oakie' Budd and himself on those occasions in the old days when his pa and he came into town to visit the sheriff and his son.

The old place brought back poignant memories which he brushed impatiently to the back of his mind. He wasn't a kid now, by heaven, as people would discover before long.

But, despite his toughness, the memories still obtruded. He remembered the stable had belonged to an old man known simply at 'Pete,' who for some unknown reason had suddenly upped and hanged himself from one of those now rotting beams above. This had happened when Frank was only a baby, but he knew the legend well. The stables were reputed to be haunted; the ghost of the suicidal old man was supposed to still lurk there of nights. A few inebriated cowboys paying the place a moonlight visit for sordid purposes claimed to have seen it, to have seen the old man creeping about, cackling, or swinging from a creaking beam, glaring eyes bulging in his bloated face. The two boys had got a delicious thrill thinking of these things as they played among the ruins and the cobwebs.

Crouching hidden there now, and peering out into the hot sunshine as if he were still playing games, Frank Carter's lips quirked in a smile that distorted his thin boyish face but did not reach his hard, man's eyes.

The place was just a tumbledown ruin that stank of filth and mould, of the urine of men and beasts, of rotting hay. He began to get restive; he relieved his pent-up feelings by shuffling his feet, by stroking the shiny barrel of his shotgun. What the hell had happened to Lafe? Wasn't he ever coming?'

There was a clatter of hooves on the hard-baked sod. Four horsemen dismounted at the Curly Cat and went inside.

Still Frank waited. The street was deserted again, bare, sordid; ribbons of shade in the cart-ruts. Bridles jingled as the horses at the hitching-rail shifted impatiently in the heat. From the Curly Cat came the hum of voices. A man laughed. Peering from cover, Frank saw faces appear at the windows, disappear again. Somebody began an amateurish clanking on the piano. A voice bawled something and the would-be musician's fingers were still again. In the stillness, Frank Carter listened in vain for the thud-thud of the hooves of an approaching horse. Those four men – maybe they had been sent out to waylay Lafe. Frank couldn't wait any longer. He had to find out some things for himself. He decided on a bold course.

He climbed into the saddle of the paint and rode him out of the stable. He kept his shotgun in the crook of his arm as he rode slowly down the street. He knew he would be spotted through the windows of the Curly Cat.

He heard a shout. Then the batwings swung. 'It's the kid!' A bunch of men, laughing and shouting, were disgorged into the street. Among them was the dark, whip-like figure of Lye Spar.

He shouted: 'Where's your pet gunman, kid? It's long past noon. Has he sent you tuh make excuses for him? The yeller rat!'

A sudden urge came over Frank – a powerful rush of feeling he was powerless to withstand – a surge of madness. He swung the shotgun.

'Watch out!' yelled one of the men. They dived for cover.

The shotgun boomed. Rolling on his stomach, Lye Spar drew and fired. Only the fact that his paint had jumped nervously saved Frank's life. He felt the wind of the slug.

Even as he pressed his knees to the horse's flanks, sending him forward, Frank discharged the other barrel of the shotgun. But Lye Spar had rolled into cover behind the batwings. Lying low over his horse's neck, Frank Carter sped out of Georgetown.

For the first half-mile the trail was deserted. Then Frank saw the two horsemen approaching. He recognized them immediately. He waved his hand.

Olly and Jim came on at a gallop and drew their horses to a halt. Their first thoughts were for the welfare of Lafe. They were shocked when they learnt he had not been in town.

Frank told them all that had transpired. He concluded by saying: 'You know that if Lafe got to town at all he'd ride straight in, he wouldn't try to sneak in.'

'Yeah, we know that,' said Jim McDougal. 'According tuh that, he couldn't have got that far—'

'Some dirty skunks musta laid fer him along the trail,' burst out Masters.

'We gotta ride back,' said Frank.

The other two men turned their horses' heads. With Frank in between them, they set off the way they had come. 'The only place along here where an ambush could be staged is at the bluffs,' said Olly Masters.

They dismounted here, and, leaving their horses tethered to a lime tree that stubbornly resisted the blazing sun, began to search.

McDougal found Lafe's hat in a clump of prickly cacti. He scratched his hands pretty badly in retrieving it. The two men and the youth looked at the dirty-grey, sweat-stained Stetson with mingled feelings. It was an ominous sign.

They split up and began to search again. It was Olly Masters who saw the body, like a bundle of rags, almost concealed by a huge boulder. With a cry that brought the others running to the spot, he dropped on his knees beside the still form.

Lafe Kramer lay on his side, his back up against the boulder, his hands behind him. His eyes were closed; there didn't seem to be any marks on him.

Olly's hand trembled slightly as he thrust it into the breast of Kramer's shirt. Then, not satisfied, he bent and put his ear to the broad chest.

'He's alive,' he said. 'He's bin doped – can't yuh smell it?'

'I thought something smelled queer,' said Jim McDougal.

'He stinks with it,' said Masters. 'They must've used plenty. An' look! His hands are lashed behind him.'

'Wal, they certainly prevented him reaching Georgetown,' said Frank. 'But I wonder why they didn't kill him an' bury him out of hand.'

'Because, so far, this method suits Judson's plans best,' said the blond McDougal. 'It suits him best to make out that Lafe's yellow; to discredit him in the eyes of a section of townspeople who're on our side.'

'Yeah, I guess you're right,' said Frank. 'He's tryin' tuh turn everybody against us.'

Masters had untied Kramer's hands. 'Help me tuh get him to a hoss,' he said. 'He's dead to the world.'

They got him to a horse and had to tie him on.

By the time they got him to the ranch he was beginning to come round. With splashings of icy water and liberal doses of whiskey, they brought him to full consciousness and listened to his tale.

When he had finished, young Frank burst out with: 'The skunks! We oughta ride intuh town an' get Judson an' Spar for good an' all—'

'You're gettin' tuh be a bloodthirsty young cuss lately, Frank,' said Kramer with a ghost of a smile.

'Whadyah want me tuh do – sit back an' let 'em do what they like with us? Kill my pa, steal my home, make a—'

'Easy, easy,' said Kramer. 'Keep your shirt on. I didn't mean it like that. We all feel the same as you do – don't we, boys?'

'Sure – sure.'

'What I mean is – that might be just what they wanted us to do: ride intuh town an' start a ruckus. If we got killed in a gun-battle which we started ourselves Judson 'ud be in the clear, wouldn't he?'

'Yeah, I guess you're right, Lafe,' said Frank. 'I'm sorry I blew up.'

'Forget it—'

'Frank started a little ruckus all on his lonesome in Georgetown,' said dark, blocky Masters, and proceeded to recount the story.

Kramer was chuckling, when he suddenly crossed to the window. 'There's riders comin',' he said. 'Four of 'em. Looks like the sheriff. Yeah, it is.'

The three men and the youth went out to meet the quartet. It consisted of the sheriff and his deputy, and the two Trouble J men – Bennett and Dobson.

The sheriff was very curt and official. He said: 'I've let your men outa jail. Nobody knows who plugged that Cross M man, an' I cain't hold 'em forever on suspicion. Big Bill Pretty's still havin' treatment for his jaw. He'll get here under his own steam when he feels like it.' The old man turned his hard gaze on the younger member of the bunch. 'So you didn't leave town right away like yuh promised, Frank. You stayed behind an' started a little private war on your lonesome.'

The other's reply held a little sneer. 'Kinda.'

'You didn't kill anybody. But you might've done,' said the sheriff. 'Right now, I'm givin' you boys warning – that's what I came here for. Keep away from Georgetown! I don't want a range war on my hands.'

'Is that an order from the law, Sheriff?' said Kramer.

'If you like to put it that way, yes – it is.'

'I gotta ride intuh Georgetown, Sheriff,' said Kramer tonelessly, and quickly recounted what had prevented him keeping his rendezvous that day at noon.

The sheriff listened him out, but betrayed no emotion. He said: 'If you come tuh Georgetown an' start any trouble, it's at your own risk, Kramer.'

The other's face was hard, his eyes slits as he looked up at the old lawman. His look betokened that if that was how the sheriff wanted it – law or no law – there was war between them from now on. That was Kramer's way. Passion surged within him, but all he said, tersely, was: 'All right, Sheriff.'

The old lawman turned his horse and set off without another word. As he followed him, Deputy Hank O'Toole called a laconic: 'So-long.'

Bennett and Dobson put their horses in the stables, then joined the little party outside the bunk-house.

'Can we get some chow, Lafe?' said Lanky Bennett to the foreman. 'Thet pesky sheriff half-starved us.'

'Yeah, sure, go an' tell Billy to rustle up somethin' for yuh.'

Billy was the Indian cook, an outcast from a wandering tribe. He slept with his squaw and papooses in a mud-roofed cabin in the small range of hills a couple of miles back and did chores at the ranch during the day. Many years back Bill Carter had saved him from drowning in a creek. Ever since then Billy, whose Indian name nobody knew, had worshipped the hard-bitten white man. What he felt about the recent killing of his mentor he did not reveal, but did his cooking and other jobs around the place with his usual silent impassive efficiency.

'What kin we do after chow, Lafe?' asked Dobson, who was an awkward, ambling cuss with a face like an amiable monkey.

'You kin help the other boys to round-up strays,' said Lafe. 'They're out by the north pastures somewheres now. The work's falling behind lately.'

'Sorry about the jail sentence,' said the lean Bennet, with a grin. 'We couldn't sit by an' hear ourselves insulted though.'

'You're darn right, yuh couldn't,' said Kramer, his face softening a little. 'Thanks for sticking out. You know we're in Dutch all round now, don't yuh?'

'Yuh kin count us in,' said Bennett.

'Yeah,' said Dobson. 'An' Big Bill, too, I guess, as soon as his jaw's mended – he's real mad to have a crack at the Cross M mob.'

SEVEN

Although the Trouble J boys knew that now anything might happen, the rest of the day and night passed uneventfully; but, with the early morning, came another bunch of horsemen – half a dozen or more Cross M men, led by Mervyn Judson, with beside him – on a horse that looked a lot too big for him – the tubby little figure of Lawyer Herbert Markson.

The sight of him, a little ludicrous in the saddle, was at least reassuring. If Judson had meant ructions, he would not have brought a lawyer along with him.

Most of the Trouble J men had ridden out on the range. Only Kramer and young Frank remained behind, as the former put it, to have an important 'pow-wow,' although both he and the younker knew without saying the real reason was in case they had visitors such as these.

The man and youth confronted the Judson mob.

The big ranch-owner – among other things – with the thick black moustache and the long jaw that made him look not unlike a vicious horse, spoke up immediately.

'Who's handlin' the business here now?'

'I handle my own business,' said Frank harshly.

'You're not old enough.'

'If that's what Frank says, that's what goes,' said Lafe Kramer. 'Whad yuh want?'

Judson made a sign to the little lawyer, who fumbled in the pocket of his cut-away coat and produced a paper. Judson took it from him and, leaning forward in the saddle, held it out to Frank. The young man reached up his good left arm and took it.

'It's an eviction notice,' said Judson. 'It's all drawn up nice an' legal. It gives you two days to get off this place.' He took another folded paper from his own pocket. 'It's drawn up in conjunction with this mortgage, which has your father's signature on it. I'm not gonna be loony enough to hand this over to yuh, but you know what's in it as well as I do – both of yuh.'

'An' if I don't get off in two days?'

'I shall have to take lawful, strong steps to have you removed.'

'Ahem,' said Lawyer Markson. 'If I may say a word – Frank, I'm here in an official capacity; there's no personal feeling on my part at all; but I must impress on you that Mr Judson can do just what he says.'

'Can he?' Frank was taking it mighty quietly.

'The ranch an' land will be legally mine in a coupla days unless you find the money in that time – an' I know you cain't,' said Judson. 'But I cain't claim the stock. However, if you want tuh do business, I'll make you a good offer for them – after I've taken the ranch, that is—'

That was the last straw. Frank Carter deliberately tore the white paper into strips. He dropped them and ground them into the sod beneath his heel.

'Get off my place,' he said.

'I came in peace—'

'Get off my place!'

Lawyer Markson looked nervously about him. 'He's had his notice. We'd better go.'

'Guess you'd better,' said Lafe Kramer. 'But before you do, *Mister* Judson, I'd like to tell you somethin'. Ambushing a man on the trail an' dopin' him ain't gonna stop you an' Spar from gettin' what's comin' to yuh. You cain't do that every time.'

'I don't know what you're talkin' about.'

'Don't yuh? Wal, jest take a message for me, will yuh? Tell your pet sidewinder Mr Lye Spar that I'll be comin' in to Georgetown in the near future. I'm not gonna give him any warnin' this time. I'm just gonna come quiet-like. When he sees me, he'd better start movin' fast, for I'm comin' a-gunnin'.'

'You'll finish up on the gallows,' said Judson pompously, for the benefit of the lawyer.

'After you, Mr Judson,' said Kramer.

The ranchman scowled and turned his horse, leading his little band back to firmer home ground.

'If only I'd had my shotgun,' said Frank.

Kramer looked at him levelly. 'Seems tuh me it's a good job for us you didn't. You cain't fight an army all on your lonesome, younker.'

Frank realized that he was right. The old, reckless Lafe had changed a little during the last few days – but somehow this new cautiousness seemed to make him even more deadly – the calm before the big storm.

The man and the youth were having a meal in the ranch-house when hooves clattered outside.

'More trouble?' snarled Kramer, springing to his feet, revealing suddenly the strain he was under whilst playing this waiting game.

Somebody thumped at the door and a voice shouted 'Frank! Lafe!'

'It's Olly Masters,' said Frank. Then he raised his voice. 'Come on in.'

The blocky cowpoke came blundering into the room. He tossed a folded news-sheet on to the table.

'Latest edition of the *Georgetown Herald*,' he said. 'There's a column on the front page you ought to read.' By the grin on Olly's dark jib it wasn't bad news, anyway,

Frank reflected, as he flipped the paper open to its full length. The headlines in question hit him between the eyes straight off. There was no doubt to whom and what they referred.

KID RANCHER SHOOTS UP THE TOWN

Frank read it aloud:

The Judson–Carter feud which has simmered perilously near boiling-point since the tragic shooting affray in which Bill Carter met his death, and bubbled again Thursday evening in the Curly Cat Saloon, came to a head again yesterday morning, when young Frank Carter took it into his head to shoot the town up . . .

Frank paused for breath. He knew this report was the work of the *Herald's* crusading editor, Mel Sterndale, who, though a capital fellow, was as long-winded in his writings as he was in his speech. The editorial continued as follows:

Young Frank took umbrage at some sneering remarks that were tossed at him by members of the Judson faction outside their stronghold, to whit, the aforesaid Curly Cat Saloon, and forthwith discharged a couple of barrels of buckshot in their direction. The fact that he did not hit any of them is deplored by this paper, which, our readers will remember, also deplored the lackadaisical verdict given by the coroner at the inquest on Frank's father, the late Mr Bill Carter, who was one of the earliest settlers in this territory, and a man of proven honesty and courage.

'Yeah, they did at that,' burst out Olly Masters. 'That

Mel Sterndale suttinly ain't afeard to speak his mind.'

'The newspaper office an' printing press is one of the few things in Georgetown Judson don't own,' said Kramer. 'When he sees this, I guess he'll wish he did.'

'I got an idea that'll maybe make him see a helluva lot more,' said young Frank suddenly. 'I gotta go see Mel Sterndale.'

'What, go intuh town?' said Kramer.

'That's where Sterndale lives, ain't it?'

'Oh, no, you don't!'

But Frank had already reached the door and opened if. It slammed almost in Kramer's face. He flung it open. Frank was already running towards the stables, but Kramer's long legs travelled faster. He caught the younker at the door of the stables.

'What's the idea, Frank?' he said.

The reply was sullen. 'I thought Mel Sterndale might like to print the full story.'

'Yeah,' said Kramer. 'That's a good idea. Why not? But that's no reason to go rampaging like a bull an' ride intuh Georgetown in broad daylight. Way things are, it ain't safe. Wait till tonight an' me an' the boys'll come with yuh.' It was a snap decision – anything to keep this reckless younker out of trouble. But, once committed, Kramer did not mean to retract. His recklessness suddenly matched Frank's. Ride in they would – and maybe make their presence felt. And to hell with Sheriff Joe Budd!

As usual, Masters and McDougal were game for anything. Inactivity irked them – the promise of action outweighed any thoughts of consequences.

Kramer told them: 'Dobson an' Bennett'll look out for things here at the ranch. Maybe I'll ask Billy tuh stay as well. The other boys'll be out night-ridin' as usual. They ain't obliged to know anythin' about our trip.'

It was about ten when the four of them started out. They knew things would still be humming in Georgetown when they got there. The night was comfortably dark, though oppressive, and with the threat of a storm in the air.

They were not crazy enough to ride directly into the town, but approached their destination – the *Herald* office and printshop – by a back route.

Mel Sterndale was alone, setting up type, when they surprised him. The movement he made towards the gun on the table near his hand was halted, and he smiled in greeting as he saw who his visitors were.

He had the usual stoop of his trade and also a paunch, which gave his short body a rather pear-like appearance. His face was ruddy, and he had little sharp blue eyes sunk in pouches of flesh above his snub nose and grim little mouth. A boyish but determined-looking character, with an idealistic passion for crusades. In his capable and fearless hands, the *Herald* was a constant goad to the less lawful elements – large and small – of Georgetown, like a burr under the saddle of a cayuse.

Straight away, young Frank Carter began his tale. Sterndale listened intently, his eyes kindling as his interest grew. In this passionate youth he sensed a kindred spirit – though mayhap not such a disciplined one, and liable to go completely haywire if not curbed. His ready pity was stirred by the boy's infirmity, but he did not show it. He knew Frank Carter would reject it with hatred were it shown. He did not need pity!

Already, as the youth talked, the little newspaperman was working out in his agile mind the high-sounding, indignant phrases of an editorial that would beat all editorials.

His round head with its thinning sandy hair kept nodding vigorously, and Frank knew he had won.

'You'll help us?'

'Need you ask, my boy?' said Sterndale. 'I'll get to work on it—'

The rest of his sentence was clipped off altogether by a harsh voice that said: 'All right, everybody! Reach fer the ceilin'.'

The Trouble J gunnies whirled, then froze. No use arguing with a battery of guns like those.

Half a dozen newcomers, with almost double that number of levelled guns among them, filed into the printshop.

'Up!' The harsh command came again from the foremost one, a wide-shouldered man with a pale face smudged by very blue jowls.

'Quite a surprise findin' you Trouble J boys here,' he said as the four cowboys and the printer elevated their hands. 'Whadyuh doing – mugging over another nasty editorial? We figured it was a put-up job.'

'What d'yuh want, Messiter?' said Sterndale.

Ralph Messiter, professional gambler and gunman, was leader of the Judson faction in town, his particular job being ramrod of all the gaming activities in Judson's various joints. He was equally cool at cards or in a fight. A mighty dangerous opponent, Lafe Kramer reflected, as he said:

'Who sent yuh here?'

'Mr Sterndale is the gentleman we came tuh visit,' said Messiter.

'Yuh meanta say you brought all these boys an' that hardware along with yuh just to see one man? Yuh don't take any chances, do yuh, Messiter?'

The thrust went home. The sudden glint in the gambler's slate-like eyes betokened that fact.

He said: 'The boys came here for a purpose. We figured Mister Sterndale an' his libellous paper are no longer of any use tuh Georgetown. I'll show yuh what I mean – Max, Jack, Pete, get tuh work—'

As the three men holstered their guns and left the group, Sterndale said: 'This sounds like Lye Spar's brand of humour.'

'Yeah,' said Messiter. 'Lye is kind of a humorous cuss, ain't he?'

Max, Jack and Pete, all burly customers, began to tip over trays of type, kicking the little metal pieces all over the stone floor.

'You skunks,' said Sterndale, starting forward.

'Easy,' said Messiter. 'I ain't playin' games.'

The little printer became still under the cold menace of those eyes, but his face revealed the anguish he was suffering at having to stand helpless while his beloved shop was wrecked.

There was a lull in the din as the wreckers stopped and looked around for further items to destroy.

A strange voice cut into the sudden stillness. It came from behind Messiter and his two pards. Ominous and commanding.

'Drop your guns, I've got yuh all covered.'

A gunman behind Messiter whirled around. The man in the back doorway did not hesitate. Smoke wreathed his fist, flame spurted as his gun crashed. With a horrible, shuddering cry, the gunny clutched at his stomach and went down.

Messiter and the other man dropped their irons as if they were red-hot, watching with awful fascination the blood that welled from their comrade's punctured hide. The three wreckers stood in ludicrous attitudes of shock and surprise.

'Up! Up!' snarled the man in the doorway. His voice, issuing from the mass of bandages that wreathed his face, had a curious sepulchral quality that was a little awe-inspiring. That, and the sight of what he had done to the man who still twitched in agony on the stone floor, were enough to make the toughest desperadoes quail.

Five pairs of hands shot up. It was turnabout with a vengeance; the paws of the other five men had already dropped to their sides.

'You're a sight for sore eyes, Bill,' said Lafe Kramer. Big Bill Pretty insinuated his huge bulk further into the shop.

'I jest finished readin' Mel's editorial, an' thought I'd like tuh pay him a visit—'

'Lucky for us yuh did,' said Sterndale.

'I'm sorry I didn't get here a mite earlier. They made a mess o' your place, Mel.'

'It'll clean up. They hadn't got to the machines yet.' Sterndale indicated the two small presses, shrouded in gloom at the other end of the shop.

The man on the floor was still now.

'Pity about him,' said Big Bill. 'Though he asked fer it – I didn't mean to do any shootin' if I could help it.'

'Yeah, you'd better get goin',' said Kramer. ' 'Fore a crowd gets here.'

'You'd all better get goin' – an' take these skunks with yuh—'

'How about you?'

'I'll be all right,' said Sterndale with a ghost of a smile. 'Power o' the press, yuh know.' His voice became urgent. 'Get goin', I say!'

'Pick up your pard! ' Kramer told Messiter and the other man. 'You three' – to the wreckers – 'take out your guns and drop 'em.'

His own guns were out now, as also were those of Masters and McDougal. The three hard cases did as they were told.

'Go out first!' ordered Kramer. 'Not too fast. An' keep it quiet. We don't want any more dead men littering the place up.'

The three men filed out the back door, Big Bill right behind them. Then came Messiter and the other man with their grisly burden, his blood staining their hands and the sleeves of their shirts.

The night was silent, except for the hum of noise that came from the Curly Cat and the other sporting-houses.

'Mebbe that shot wasn't heard,' said Frank.

'Yeah, quite possible,' said Kramer.

'What do we do with these birds?' said Big Bill.

For a moment the Trouble J foreman did not answer. Then he said reflectively: 'I got an idea. Keep moving – towards the back o' the Curly Cat. Would you like to slip on in front, Frank, an' see if the coast's clear?'

'Shore, Lafe.' The younker slid off into the blanketing darkness. He soon vanished.

'What's the game?' panted Messiter.

'You'll find out,' said Kramer. Then he turned to Jim McDougal and whispered: 'Fetch the hosses.'

Messiter's pard, who was helping him to carry the body, began to retch. He was not as tough as he pretended to be. Kramer, who didn't seem to have any feelings at all, told him to shut up.

Frank joined them as they reached the back of the Curly Cat.

'They're rippin' up the floor in there,' he said, 'but there's nothin' doin' at the back at all.'

'Stick the body in that old privy over there,' said Kramer with sardonic humour.

Messiter and his pard did as they were told. The latter was trembling as if he had ague. The three other Judson hard cases stood woodenly.

Kramer gave his orders to Frank, Big Bill, Masters, and McDougal. 'Take these four bozoes out on the range – right out – an' lose 'em. They can walk back tuh town, an' I don't want 'em tuh get here till tomorrow morning.'

Mounted now, the three men and the youth shepherded the Judson men in front of them.

'Get goin',' said Kramer.

'How about you, Lafe?' said Frank.

'Don't worry about me, kid. I got a little unfinished business tuh tend to. I'll foller yuh.'

EIGHT

That night the Curly Cat was even fuller than usual. The morning had brought on the stage coach from Santa Fe half a dozen new girls – real beauties. They were the chorus who were to back Milly La Moure in her song-and-dance act. The show was scheduled for eleven – Mervyn Judson knew that was the ideal time to get a really receptive audience. Promptly at that time the curtain that screened the small stage slowly parted. A cheer went up, all gaming and jigging was forgotten as everybody's necks were craned in that same direction.

Miss Milly, the belle of the Curly Cat, and Mervyn Judson's own particular property, tripped on to the stage. More cheers went up and a storm of clapping.

Milly's shapely form was dressed in a long, spangled gown. Her golden hair framed her pretty oval face like a halo, sparkling beneath the lights. To these roughs who applauded her she was no ordinary song-and-dance girl, she was a 'lady,' Mervyn Judson's own particular lady, and they called her 'Miss Milly.' She ruled them like a queen, and even the most hard-bitten of them gloried in it.

Behind that doll-like façade was purpose and ruthlessness. Born in an Eastern slum, her real name Milly Schnieder, brought West when only a child, her parents were killed in a cattle stampede. She was the mistress of a wealthy ranchman when she was sixteen. She left him and went on the stage. That was when Judson saw her – at the Royale Theatre in San Antonio. He offered her a job as hostess of the Curly Cat. That was three years ago. Right now, Milly's position there was stronger than ever. She was Judson's biggest drawing card and, rumour had it, much more besides. But what the poker-faced man really thought about her nobody really knew – except perhaps Milly herself, and she was notoriously close-mouthed. They were both gamblers – both with their eyes wide open for the main chance.

Milly began to sway her hips and sing. It was a new, slow, sentimental number from back East – just the right sort for her clear, slightly husky voice. There was a lot of lovin' and kissin' in it, and Milly made it as suggestive as possible by rolling her eyes and smiling archly every time she paused a little. The hoodlums lapped it up with delighted cries.

Then the chorus came on, amid whistles. They were clad in very abbreviated tights and not much else, except white ten-gallon hats. Say, ol' Merv shore knew how tuh put a show on. Yippee!

Milly did the swaying and the singing, and the girls did the high-kicking – that's what they were there for.

Milly swung into a chorus song. The girls joined in. Milly blew kisses to the audience, shouting: 'All together – everybody!'

With much banging of the tables and stamping of feet, everybody took up the chorus. The music was supplied by piano, two violins, banjo, and the inevitable bull-fiddle. For a time they were drowned by the raucous voices. Percentage-girls going the rounds with more liquor got plenty of trade for more than liquor. And more than one dollar bill was shoved down the top of a tight silk stocking as one of the bedizened beauties sat on the knee of a bawling cowboy.

The air was thick, the lights shone fuggily through a

blue haze. The faro dealers and roulette gents wore long faces and the barmen beamed.

Amid a storm of cheering Milly and her girls ran from the stage. There were loud groans as the curtains slowly closed.

Milly stuck her head out cheekily. 'More later on, folks,' she carolled.

She knew they would wait. And tonight the Curly Cat would certainly lick the cream – plenty of it! She exchanged a nod with Lye Spar, who stood against the bar and looked a mite happier than usual. She loathed the little skunk, but it was her policy to be nice to everybody. It paid better dividends. She saw Deputy O'Toole drinking quietly by himself and, as always when she saw the law, she stiffened and became suspicious – but, hell, even a lawman was entitled to have a quiet drink now and then.

It sure would be a gala night tonight, she told herself again. It was – but not in the way that Milly expected.

The scene was set. The chief actor came through the batwings and on to the perilous stage he had chosen for himself. There was a clear space by the doorway, and he was not noticed until he had crossed this. Then somebody exclaimed: 'Here's Lafe Kramer!'

Heads turned, bodies instinctively moved out of his path. The word passed along to Lye Spar at the bar. Only he remained where he was as people moved away from him as if he had the plague. He merely turned with his back to the bar and came away a little to face his enemy.

There was a wide arena now and silence. And a space of the floor between the two men, on which stood a small, lone, round table with an empty glass and a jumbled deck of cards.

'Howdy, Lye,' said Kramer. 'Sorry I'm kinda late for muh appointment. Got held up.'

'Don't mention it, Lafe.'

Both actors spoke their lines well. It was all in the tradition. And the audience watched and listened with bated breath.

Kramer said: 'Neat little trick you pulled, Lye. Cain't see your object, though – yuh know I'd get here sooner or later.'

Spar said: 'What are yuh talkin' about, Lafe? What d'yuh want?'

Kramer said: 'You know what I want, an' yuh know what I'm talkin' about, but, for the benefit of anybody who don't understand, I'll tell it. I had a date with you at noon – everybody knows about that. I meant tuh keep it. Figuring to make me out a yeller dawg, you had some o' your boys waylay me at the buttes an' dope me—'

Spar's thin lips curled in a sneer. 'What a cock-eyed story. Still, you always were one tuh make things up an' talk too much.' He was tensed, waiting.

'I ain't talkin' no more,' said Kramer. He crouched a little, letting his long body go stack; but his arms ceased to dangle and were crooked so that his clawed hands hovered over the twin butts of his guns. His cold grey eyes became slits, shutting out all light, all vision, except the figure before him of the man he meant to kill – a figure that was crouching, too. Little, dark, monkey-like, like a bunch of coiled springs.

Then a voice rapped out: 'There'll be no gunfight while I'm here.'

Kramer's eyes widened as another figure moved into view. Spar straightened as Hank O'Toole moved along the bar beside him.

'Hallo, Hank,' said Kramer.

The deputy's good-natured face was hard. He said: 'Yuh were told tuh keep away from town, Lafe. You were told not to come here causin' trouble agin.' He took a couple of steps forward 'You'd better come with me tuh the office, Lafe.'

Kramer's eyes narrowed again. His talon-like hands did

not change their position. He was ominously still in the crouch of a born gunfighter – ready to spit sudden death.

'Stay right there, Hank,' he said. 'You cain't stop me now. This is between me an' Spar, an' it's gotta be settled once an' for all.'

A look of pain flitted into O'Toole's blue eyes.

'Don't make it hard for me, pard,' he said.

'Stay still!'

O'Toole froze, but his eyes blazed now. 'All right – reach! An' be damned tuh yuh!'

He was lined up beside Spar now, watchful and alert.

Kramer realized he had lost a friend now and gained another opponent. If that's how the cards were stacked, they'd have to stay that way. He was pretty confident that he could beat either of the two men singly; but could he beat them both together? Two shots. One for each. And if he failed – nothing to worry about any more. A little smile creased his saturnine face as he made his decision.

What happened next surprised everybody. A shotgun boomed, a window was burst inwards. The hanging lamp behind O'Toole and Spar was smashed to fragments. The other one, before the stage, disintegrated, too, as a second barrel was discharged. Darkness fell like a physical blow. Women screamed, men shouted hoarsely.

Kramer moved fast. In a second he was outside and had turned a corner. The barrel of the shotgun glinted as Frank Carter met him. He held the reins of Kramer's horse. His own paint pony followed dutifully in the rear.

Without a word between them, both men mounted, kneed their horses forward. Frank was reloading in the saddle. They were turning the corner when a shot sounded from inside the building, and a gurgling cry of agony.

'Sounds like somebody hit the wrong man,' said Kramer.

As they galloped past, Frank elevated the shotgun and

fired, sending a screaming charge into the log walls. There was an almighty scuffling inside and a chorus of shouts and oaths. Kramer heard the young man chuckling to himself.

They were out on the trail before the foreman spoke. 'What made you come back?'

'I figured out what you might be doin' an' that you'd probably need help, so I sent the boys on—'

'Thanks, pardner,' said Kramer. He stuck out a hand. 'Looks like you saved my bacon.'

Frank had a grip on his left hand like the clutch of a vice. He said: 'You could've beat them two, but there might've been others.'

'Maybe I could,' said Kramer; 'but one of 'em was Hank O'Toole, an' I like Hank.'

'He stuck his neck out,' said Frank curtly.

The bar-room of the Curly Cat was illuminated once more as willing though rather nervous hands took lanterns from the two bartenders.

Lye Spar still stood in his original position. A few yards in front of him lay the small table, overturned, the glass smashed, the cards strewn across the boards.

Hank O'Toole was tangled up with the legs of the table. He was lying on his face, the top of his head, with the ruffled corn-coloured hair, up against the underside of the table. He was very still. His hat was rumpled at his side, his hands out each side of him, the fingers half-clenched, as if he had grabbed at the table to stop himself falling and so brought it over. As the nearest onlookers took in the garish scene they noticed a trickle of red, a splash here and there – over the playing cards, but having nothing to do with their design.

Then a girl cried out, half a sob, half a scream.

'Lye,' said somebody. 'What's happened to Hank?'

The Judson *segunda* left the bar and bent over O'Toole. With a hand at his shoulder, he turned him over.

'That shot,' he said. 'It hit Hank plumb in the heart – I guess Kramer got one of us after all.'

'Here's the sheriff,' said somebody, and Joe Budd strode to the centre of the fateful arena.

'What's all the shooting about?' Then he saw his deputy.

'Hank,' he gasped, and fell on his knees beside his friend.

'Ain't nothin' you can do, Sheriff,' said Spar.

The old man raised his head, a look in his grey eyes that made even the callous gunman quiver.

'Who done it?'

'Lafe Kramer.'

Disbelief shone in the eyes, then the sheriff rose.

'Let's hear everythin',' he said.

'What's goin' on?' said another voice harshly, and Mervyn Judson came through from behind the bar.

'Lafe Kramer killed O'Toole,' said Spar.

The saloon-owner's poker-face did not change, but his eyes gleamed.

He said: 'I thought it wuz him an' the kid I passed on the trail.'

'Let's hear it all,' said the sheriff. Heavy lids shielded his eyes, masking his grief. His voice was very harsh. He listened as Spar, helped by others, recounted the tale. When they had finished, he said:

'So none of you saw Kramer shoot Hank. It might've bin anybody in the dark.'

'It couldn't've bin anybody else,' said Lye Spar. 'Kramer was facin' Hank. It looked like Hank dived for him as the lights went out an' Kramer shot him.'

'They wuz pards.'

'Not after the way Hank challenged Kramer. He didn't mean to back down to him. If it didn't happen like I said,' added Spar, 'maybe Kramer was takin' a shot at where he figured I'd be, an' he hit Hank instead.'

'Let me see your guns,' said Joe Budd.

'Why, Sheriff. Yuh don't think I—?'

'I gotta check up. Let me see 'em.'

Spar shrugged. He whipped out his guns and clapped them on the bar.

The sheriff scrutinized them. 'All right,' he said. 'They ain't bin fired. Thought maybe you might've shot at Kramer an' hit Hank instead.'

'Nice of yuh to be so straight about it,' said Spar with a sneer. 'But if I'd fired I should've hit Hank in the back. Anybody'll tell yuh I wuz a little ways behind him.'

Many voices backed the little gunny. And there wasn't much doubt, either, that everybody figured Lafe Kramer had done the shooting.

The sheriff said: 'Will some of yuh see that Hank's body is taken tuh the undertaker's. I'm ridin' tuh the Trouble J.'

'We'll come with yuh,' said an old-timer. 'We'll lynch the skunk.'

'I'm goin' alone,' said the sheriff. 'I'll do this my own way. Hank wuz my pard as well as my deputy. All of yuh stay here, y' understand?'

'But, Sheriff, Kramer's dangerous.'

'Let me worry about that.'

'You oughta have a posse.'

'I've told yuh – I'm goin' alone. Stay here, all of yuh.'

'If that's the way the sheriff wants it, you'd all better do as he says,' said Mervyn Judson.

Joe Budd began to walk towards the door but turned, as did every head in the room, as shouts rang out from the back. A white-faced man burst through the door that separated the bar-room from the rest of the building.

'Boss! Sheriff! Homer Larrabee's bin shot. He's out back – in the old privy – blood all over the place—'

'Good heavens! How—?'

'I think I can explain all about that little matter, Sheriff,' said a clear, calm voice.

All eyes were turned upon Mel Sterndale, editor of the *Georgetown Herald*.

'Don't go, Mr Spar,' rapped Mel.

Lye Spar stopped in his tracks and turned. 'What's eatin' yuh?' he snarled.

Masters, McDougal, and Big Bill Pretty joined Bennett, Dobson, and Billy the Indian at the Trouble J. Billy was told he could go home to his squaw and papooses if he wanted to. Billy was very fond of his family, so he went. The others gathered in the bunk-house.

'Riders comin',' said Masters suddenly. McDougal blew out the lamp.

As one man, they dropped their hands to their guns as they stood in the darkness listening.

Then McDougal said: 'Sounds like Frank and Lafe.'

'Yeah; it does,' said Big Bill. 'I kin tell the galloping o' that paint o' the kid's.'

The two riders dismounted outside. Big Bill went to the door.

'It's them all right.'

McDougal relit the lamp as the two of them entered.

'Get ready tuh douse it again,' rapped Kramer. 'There may be a mob after us.'

'Let 'em come,' said Big Bill. His vehemence hurt his jaw. He swore and clapped a hand to it.

Kramer said: 'Wal, boys, what did you do with Mr Ralph Messiter an' his stick-up boys?'

Olly Masters chuckled. 'We took 'em out as far as Devil's Canyon,' he said. 'Made 'em run all the way – last part of it on their knees.'

'Gosh,' said Kramer, 'they won't be back tuh town by tomorrer night if they've got to leg it from there. Good fer you, boys. Now I guess you'd like to hear my own news – an' Frank's, the young bobcat.'

He told his tale succinctly. Frank was congratulated on

all sides. He took the demonstration with immobile calm, a little smile on his thin face. They weighed him up, and rightly – a queer kid and a mighty dangerous one. He didn't seem like the quiet cripple boy they had known and faintly pitied. They accepted him now as a desperate equal.

'That O'Toole,' growled Big Bill, who, despite his jaw, kept gabbing. 'The damn' fool.'

'Look, boys,' said Kramer. 'We gotta get prepared. But there's no need to lose sleep. We'll take turns in pairs to stand guard.'

This scheme was agreed upon by all present. The monkey-faced Dobson produced a pack of cards and they cut for first turn on guard. It fell to Dobson's pard, the lanky Bennett, and blond Jim McDougal.

Kramer and Frank imbibed the hot coffee that Billy had left on the stove for them, then dossed down with the others. Bennett and McDougal went out to the stables.

Snores floated gently out to the two men as they smoked and watched. But the happy ear-pounders were not to be left in peace for long.

McDougal's cigarette stub cut a glittering arc in the black night and he said: 'Somethin's comin'.' He had ears like a lynx. 'I cain't hear anythin',' said Bennett. 'Wait a minute.' He got down on his knees and pressed his ears to the ground.

He looked up. 'Yeah, you're right.'

'We'd better warn the others,' said McDougal.

When Sheriff Budd reined in his horse the bunk-house light was on again, and a reception committee awaited. They were mighty puzzled at seeing him alone, seeing the haggard look on his face when he came through the door.

He wasted no time in greeting, but said:

'I've come tuh take you in, Lafe Kramer – for the murder tonight of my deputy, Hank O'Toole.'

In the stunned silence that followed, he spoke again. 'And you, Bill Pretty, for the killing of Homer Larrabee.

There's some excuse fer you, but none for Kramer – none at all!'

Then the babel broke out, everybody talking at once.

Kramer's voice silenced it. 'Wait a minute.' He looked at the sheriff. 'I didn't kill Hank O'Toole. Everybody here 'cept you knows that, Joe. I didn't fire a shot tonight. This is a plant of some kind. Have you got a mob behind yuh, creepin' up on us while you keep us talkin', Sheriff?'

'I'm alone,' said Joe Budd.

'The shot, Lafe,' broke in Frank with an excitement that was unusual for him. 'The shot we heard when we were ridin' away – an' somebody cried out. That must've bin when Hank wuz killed. You were outside with me. You couldn't've done it.'

'Of course I couldn't've done it. This is another Judson plant. Or, more likely, a Lye Spar one – he could've plugged Hank easy.'

'Spar's guns hadn't bin fired,' said the sheriff. His voice was toneless. 'I don't believe you meant tuh kill Hank, Lafe. You came tuh kill Spar, and you didn't mean tuh leave without doing it. When the younker shot the lights out – it was you, wasn't it, Frank?'

'It was.'

'In the dark, you took a potshot at Spar and hit Hank instead.'

'You believe all that? Did you look at everybody's guns. Anybody there could've shot him. My guns haven't bin fired, either.' Kramer's draw was lightning-quick, his twin Colts pointed at the lawman's chest.

The old man's face got bleaker, but he did not move. Kramer smiled thinly and spun the guns in his hands. He handed them butt-foremost to the sheriff. 'See fer yourself.'

The old man held them, his fingers curling around the triggers. He did not attempt to inspect them. He said 'You've had plenty o' time tuh fix that.' He jerked one gun meaningly. 'C'mon, Lafe, we've gotta ride. Don't start anythin' or I'll have no hesitation in shooting you with one of your own guns.'

'You crazy ol' fool,' snarled Kramer. 'I could've killed yuh then. D'yuh think I'd've taken a chance like that if I'd really killed Hank? Give me those guns back an' let's talk this thing over.'

'We'll do that back in Georgetown,' said the sheriff. 'You'd better come along, too, Big Bill.'

The giant with the bandage around his jaw grunted and began to walk forward. He screened Frank Carter from the sheriff's gaze. The younker reached swiftly beneath a bunk and brought forth his shotgun.

Big Bill stopped walking.

'All right, Mr Budd,' said Frank. 'Drop them guns.'

For a moment the old man and the youngster looked at each other.

There was no mercy in the pinched face and cold eyes of the kid as he said: 'There's too many of us here, Mr Budd. Better drop 'em.'

The sheriff's voice sounded old and tired as he replied: 'I wouldn't want tuh shoot you, Frank.'

He let the guns slide from his big hands. They hit the floor with a clatter that was deafening in the quiet room. He looked at the faces around him. They all seemed cast in the same hard, merciless mould.

He turned slowly. His huge shoulders seemed to droop as he walked to the door. He opened it and passed out. Nobody moved until the sound of his horse's hooves were fading across the yard.

'Thanks again, Frank,' said Lafe.

'Forget it.'

'The Shotgun Kid!' ejaculated Big Bill. The remark did not sound as jocular as he had intended.

NINE

Sheriff Budd rode hard. His mind was stultified and he felt deadly tired. He drove his horse with a frenzy, but inside of him there was nothing.

Although it was late when he got to Georgetown, knots of men were still hanging around. They were quiet, in an atmosphere of strain and waiting. They erupted when they saw the sheriff.

'Yuh didn't get 'em!' 'What happened?' 'Yuh didn't get the skunks!'

He ignored them and rode on, dismounting outside his own frame bungalow. He was a widower and lived there with his son, Oakland. The youth was not at home. His bedclothes were thrown back, hanging on to the floor as if he had got out in a hurry.

When the sheriff left earlier that night, he had thought Oak was still sleeping; usually he was a pretty heavy sleeper. But evidently he had heard the ruckus, too, and gone out to investigate; and, the old man knew, to help his dad if he could.

Or, then again, maybe he was out the back or something. The sheriff went out to look. Oak was all he had left now. Hank was gone. For a moment the grief was like a physical pain that made him feel weak and ill.

Sweat beaded his forehead as he opened the back door. A blast of air from the wind-blown range pulled him round a bit. He leaned against the jamb of the door and called softly: 'Oak, you there, Oak? Oak!'

There was no answer. From out front, down the street, came a subdued clamour of voices.

The sheriff went back to the kitchen and lit the lamp. He opened a cupboard and, bringing forth a bottle of whiskey, uncorked it and took a deep swig. It took his breath away and made him cough.

He put the bottle back. Now he felt better. He squared his massive shoulders and hitched up his gunbelt. A faintly sardonic smile crossed his lined face. Not that his guns seemed any good to him lately.

He went out front again. He left his horse where he stood and proceeded down the road to the office on foot.

There was a lot of chatter going on down by the Curly Cat, and the clattering of restive horses. Right now, Joe Budd wasn't even interested. He had to find his son.

But he started as a voice bawled: 'All right! Let's go!'

There was a chorus of yells, then the sound of many galloping horses. The sheriff paused irresolute. He was outside his office now. There was no light there. The door was locked. He had thought maybe Oak would be there.

He paused again. Then he produced his key, unlocked the door and entered. The office felt cold. He struck a match, lit the lamp mechanically, and looked about him. No, it didn't seem like Oak had been here. He wouldn't be doing anything out back, surely? There wasn't even a drunk in the cells.

'Oak!' he called. 'You around, Oak?'

Feet clattered, and his cry was answered from the doorway.

'Dad.' Oak was panting. 'Dad. Lye Spar's leadin' a mob of men out tuh Frank's place. Dad, cain't yuh do somethin'? Cain't yuh stop 'em?'

'There's nothin' I kin do now, son,' said the sheriff quietly.

*

The Trouble J men were still debating when they heard the dull thrum of the approaching horses.

'Gosh, it ain't took 'em long,' said Dobson.

'Wal, boys,' said Kramer. 'Looks like our minds've bin made up for us. Whadyuh vote we do – make a run fer it?'

'Fight 'em!' said Big Bill Pretty.

His definite conclusion was backed up unanimously. Kramer smiled thinly. They hadn't needed that goad about making a run for it, but he said:

'Frank's boss here now. We'll do as he says.'

'We'll fight,' said Frank without hesitation, and in his queer, cold-blooded way he seemed quite happy about it.

'Wal, you've suttinly got a mighty salty bunch of hellions tuh back yuh up,' said the foreman. 'All right, boys. We ain't got much time. Pull the bunks down. Block the windows, all except for peepholes. An' the kitchen door and window, too. Better shove the kitchen table agin' that door. An' this table against this one. They're weak spots, the doors are. Have we got plenty ammunition?'

'Plenty,' said Olly Masters. 'All the ammunition an' guns the ranch owns are in here, I guess. We'll give 'em a run for their money.' Kramer ran to give him help with the big table.

The bunk-house was a long, squat place, built entirely of thick logs. It had only one door, with a low window each side of it. The small kitchen was a lean-to at the side, reached by another door that was always open. The kitchen was made of logs, too, and had a small door and a small high window.

Big Bill, who seemed to have forgotten his busted jaw entirely in his excitement at the thoughts of another fight, worked single-handed in this little lean-to. He upended the stout deal table against the door, which, being only boards, was a weak spot; then he carted a bunk from the other room and blocked the window with it, leaving a loophole at one side. He fetched his rifle and loaded it. Then he looked to his two guns.

He was satisfied. He shouted: 'I'll look after this end.'

'All right,' said Kramer.

The furniture-moving ceased. The men were satisfied. The place looked like an armed fort.

'All set, boys? Got all your guns an' ammunition to hand?' said Kramer.

There was an affirmative chorus. Young Frank patted his beloved shotgun.

'All right,' said the foreman. 'I'll put the light out, then we can see 'em better as they approach.'

He puffed and, as if it were a signal, darkness fell like a pitch-black blanket. Kramer felt his way across the room and, rifle in hand, joined Frank at the window.

'How d'yuh feel, younker?'

'Fine,' was the laconic reply.

The thud of approaching hooves sounded very much nearer. The watchers strained their eyes, peering through loopholes into the darkness outside. They began to see more clearly vague suggestions of familiar things. The stable door; the end of the stable; the corral fence; the old wagon with a broken wheel; the water butt; the stump in the ground, all that was left of an old tree – perhaps only Frank, Kramer and Bill remembered that tree in its prime. Frank because he was born at this ranch, Kramer and Pretty because they were the oldest hands.

'Here they come,' said the lynx-eyed Jim McDougal, who, although his hair was blond, had all the attributes of a wild Indian – and very few of his vices.

Horses clattered, drew to a slithering halt. The watchers could vaguely define the shapes of the mounted men. There were a lot of them.

'Lemme shoot a load into the middle of 'em,' said Frank.

Kramer laid a cautionary hand on his arm. 'Hold it a mite.' Then he raised his voice in a shout: 'Halloa! What d'yuh want?'

The men inside the bunk-house heard muttered exclamations, then the voice of Lye Spar replied: 'We want you, Kramer, an' Bill Pretty. You'd better come out right away; it'll save a lotta trouble. We're gonna get yuh, anyway, but we don't want to hurt anybody else if we can help it.'

'Gettin' soft-hearted, ain't yuh, Lye?' bawled Olly Masters.

'Go tuh hell!' yelled Kramer.

The others seemed to hold a quick consultation. Then the mass of figures broke and began to disintegrate into separate pieces, going in all directions – seeking cover. Frank Carter pressed the trigger of his shotgun.

The report in the confined space of the bunk-house was like a cannon going off. The charge screamed into the night. A horse shrilled, a man shouted hoarsely with pain. The dark figures began to bob around frenziedly. Spears of flame began to bob around them. Bullets thumped into the solid logs of the bunkhouse, smashed the windows, and were stopped by the barricades, except for one lucky shot that found a loophole and whined like an angry insect in the confined space until it hit the back wall.

Where the milling horsemen had been was just blue emptiness, except for a single tottering shape.

'Looks like one of 'em's hit,' said Bennett.

Two more men ran out of cover to the aid of the staggering one. Kramer took careful aim with his Winchester and dropped one of them in the dust with a bullet in his leg. The two wounded men and the other one dragged themselves into cover, then the fusillade began.

'Keep your heads down,' yelled Kramer.

He knew that now the attackers realized the Trouble J men meant business they would keep in cover and try to wear the defence down. It was a good job he had thought about those barricades. The deck was stacked against them now, and there was no drawing back. He knew there wasn't a man who wanted to draw back, anyway. They were real salty trouble-shooters. Bill Carter had picked his men well.

Big Bill Pretty's rifle boomed in the small kitchen as he fired at two men who ran for the cover of the stables. He cursed as he missed in the trick darkness. The bulk of the attackers were hiding around the corner of the further-most end of the stables. Others were crouched behind miscellaneous objects – inevitable ranch rubble that bestrewed the yard. Their horses were a tight, milling bunch by the corner post of the corral.

Most of the defence opened up at dark shapes flitting along behind the bars and slats of the corral fence. The shapes vanished as they flopped down like puppets; but whether any of them were hit was hard to determine. The defenders strained their eyes.

Jim McDougal fired at the dim, snake-like figure of a man crawling along on his belly. The figure lay still. Scattered firing broke out now from all the attackers. There wasn't a full pane of glass left in the bunk-house windows, but the upended bunks that blocked them stopped the slugs. From behind this cover the defenders opened up, too, and the night was a hideous cacophony, a rolling blatter of shooting that echoed and re-echoed, the whining whistle of slugs ricochetting into the night, the cry of frightened horses and the curses and shouts of savage men.

During the lull Kramer said: 'Don't waste your ammunition, boys. Wait till you can see something to shoot at.'

'That's right, Lafe,' shouted Big Bill, who, on his perch at the little kitchen window, had the best sniping position of all, and was still trying to get a good shot at the two men skulking in the stables.

'All I can see is durned shadows,' said Dobson plaintively.

'Quit belly-aching, yuh pug-faced skunk,' said his pard,

the lanky Bennett. 'Here – have a swig o' this.'

Dobson took a swig from the bottle and passed it along the line. It was raw, fiery whiskey.

'Hey, how about me?' bawled Bill Pretty from the kitchen.

The firing was desultory now, the slugs thudding harmlessly into the logs and barricades. Bottle in hand, Bennett ran across the big room towards the kitchen door. He never reached it. He gave a strangled cry. His long body hit the floor with a thud. The whiskey bottle smashed into fragments.

Dobson threw himself across the boards to his pard. 'Cal! Where yuh hit?'

'In the side – high up.' Bennett's voice was strangled and soft.

Lafe Kramer crawled across the floor. 'We'll hafta have a light,' he said 'Keep low, all of yuh!'

Frank Carter followed him and got the lantern. They got it down on the floor beside Bennett, whose breath was coming from him in harsh gasps that seemed to be tearing his body to pieces, making the others wince as they heard them. Kramer lit the lamp.

'I'll shield it,' said Frank, and he got down between the lamp and windows. It lit up the white, sweat-bedewed face of the wounded man, and the puckered, anxious monkey-face of Dobson. He said: 'Mebbe if we got him on a bunk—'

'Too risky tuh move him,' said Kramer. He turned the wounded man gently. 'Easy, Cal.'

A faint groan was forced between the lean man's teeth. He was bleeding freely.

'I want plenty o' cloth,' said Kramer. He felt Bennett shudder beneath his hand. Dobson was watching the white face. 'Cal!' he said.

Kramer took his hand slowly away. 'Nothin'll be any help now,' he said.

Bennett and Dobson had been like twins. The latter's monkey-face was puckered with grief. 'The buzzards,' he said. 'The buzzards.' Then he turned and went back to his post.

Olly Masters helped Kramer to carry Bennett to the back of the bunk-house. They covered him up with a blanket, then Kramer blew out the lamp.

The air was full of the fumes of whiskey and the biting smell of cordite. Gunsmoke rasped the throat and made the eyeballs smart and water.

Bill Pretty's rifle boomed in the kitchen, and the big man croaked savagely in his bandages as a man rolled into the doorway of the stables and lay still.

'One for Cal,' he said softly.

He knew there was only one man in there now. He held his fire and waited.

Frank said: 'I wonder what's happened tuh the two night-riders?'

Kramer said: 'They've probably high-tailed it. Yuh cain't blame them, I guess.'

These two men were fresh hands on the Trouble J who had elected to do night guards. Bill Carter had set them on about three weeks before he died. They were gunnies hired for that purpose, in case if rustlers. But this was not their fight.

Frank cradled his shotgun and let fly. He thought he heard a cry. At this time, when the darkness made straight shooting difficult, his weapon was probably the most devastating of the lot.

He started back as a slug buzzed through an aperture and nearly took his ear off. Up along the line Jim McDougal gave an agonized curse.

Questions were flung at him. 'Jest my arm,' he said, then added, with a humour that was unusual for him, 'I got another one.'

'They're gettin' closer,' said Dobson as he sniped at a

running figure which rolled into cover. He didn't know whether he had hit it or not.

Bill Pretty saw a shadow move in the stables, and let fly once more. The shadow became still. Big Bill waited.

The attackers were pouring in fire from all sides, covering themselves as they tried to advance. The Trouble J men fired at moving shadows. The lean figure of a man rose suddenly from behind an overturned cart as if jerked upwards on a string, then flopped again. The shadows became still.

'That's stopped 'em!' said Olly Masters jubilantly.

Like his pards, he began to reload. There was a pause in the firing of the other side as well.

The voice of Lye Spar rang out: 'Better give up, you men. You ain't got a chance. We'll get you all, sooner or later. Better give yourselves up. All we want is Kramer an' Pretty. We don't mean to harm anybody else!'

'Horse-feathers!' jeered Olly Masters.

Big Bill Pretty's answer was another shot, and the second man in the stables, who had gotten careless in the quietness, bit the dust.

Savage firing broke out once more. Peering into the darkness, the Trouble J men retaliated at the flashes that lit the night intermittently.

While Kramer was binding the flesh wound in McDougal's arm with a strip torn from the tall, blond man's shirt, the latter's pard – blocky Masters – cursed in agony as a bullet smashed his fingers.

He silenced the anxious questions with blistering curses that betokened he was still very much alive.

McDougal said softly: 'They're findin' the chinks now. I'll be all right, Lafe, allus was handier with a Colt, anyway. Go see tuh Olly.'

Kramer crawled towards Masters, a squat, crouching shape in the darkness.

Dobson's rifle kicked in his hands. 'Another one fer you, Cal,' he said softly.

'They're tryin' tuh get round the back of us,' said Jim McDougal.

As he was binding Masters's hand, Kramer said: 'If they do, we're really boxed in. We're wittling 'em down, but I guess we're still outnumbered purty near three tuh one. An' our ammunition won't last forever.'

'Maybe we oughta make a run for it while there's still a chance. If they attack from the other side, we'll be really hawg-tied,' said McDougal.

'Maybe we had,' said Kramer. 'What do you say about it, Frank? It's up tuh you, boy.'

The younker was silent for a moment. Then he said: 'Unless we want tuh stop here an' get picked off one by one, I guess we gotta make a try for it—'

'Here they come again!' yelled Dobson.

In the kitchen, Big Bill gave a wild whoop.

'That'll do, Lafe, thanks,' said Olly Masters. He raised the Colt in his other hand.

Above everything else, Frank's shotgun boomed intermittently. The place was full of swirling gunsmoke.

Even after the firing had died down again, the men's heads sang with the reverberations. They cursed as the smoke stung their eyes and throats.

'They're lying low again,' said Kramer. 'We gotta figure somethin' out—'

The raucous voice of Lye Spar broke in on his soliloquy: 'You listenin' in there?'

'We're listenin'!' replied the Trouble J straw-boss.

'We're givin' yuh one more chance. Come out with your hands up. If yuh don't, we're gonna smoke yuh out.'

'Go tuh hell!' said Kramer.

A silence ensued. Frank said 'I've got an idea.'

'Yeah? Spill it. 'Pears like we need one right now.'

'There's a back way tuh the stables – a couple o' loose boards that swing aside – I useter use it when I didn't want pa tuh know I wuz goin' in there. There's enough room to get a hoss through. All I gotta do is dodge out the back door. Them bozoes at the front won't see me, an' it don't look like any of 'em 'uv got that far round yet. Anyway, Big Bill kin cover me—'

'It's mighty risky,' said Kramer: 'I'll have a crack at it—'

Frank's voice cracked out. 'If anybody's gonna do it, it'll be me. I know where the loose boards are – an' I know my way around that stable blindfold. Anybody else might ball it up—'

'They're lightin' a torch,' said Jim McDougal.

'We ain't got no more time to argue,' said Frank. 'I'm goin'. Big Bill'll cover me from the door while I bring the hosses out. Keep up a red-hot fire from here so as nobody gets a chance to investigate.'

'All right, Frank,' said Kramer.

Frank left his shotgun – it would just be a burden now – and, unarmed, went into the kitchen. Big Bill swung the table away from the door and opened it a crack.

'All right?' whispered Frank.

'Looks that way.' Big Bill flung the door wide, taking a desperate chance as his huge form was silhouetted in the opening. His Colts gleamed in his hands.

Nothing happened. The bunkhouse seemed to rock as the Trouble J boys opened up in earnest. The attackers' first flaming torch traced a fiery trail in the air and fell in front of the door. It spluttered harmlessly.

Crouching low, Frank ran across the few yards of ground that separated the kitchen from the stables. With the ease of long practise, he swung aside the boards and stepped into the darkness beyond. He stood for a second listening. In here the shooting sounded muffled. The horses moved nervously. He saw their faint outlines in the gloom. In the doorway of the stables a man lay sprawled on his face. A little way away from this one Frank could see the motionless feet of another one, the rest of him was hidden in the shadows. Something glinted in front of him – the gun that had spun from his hand.

Frank figured he had nothing to fear from those two bozoes. He dealt with his own paint pony first, sending him through the gap on his own. He knew the faithful beast would wait patiently outside, as he had done on many nights before.

He was leading the third horse through the gap when some instinct made him turn. The protruding feet were moving; a hand and an arm joined them, reaching for the gun in the straw.

Frank leapt across the intervening space and, even as the wounded man's hand closed over the gun, swung his foot. The heavy boot crunched against the white patch which was the man's face. The man gave a little cry. The hand and arm vanished again and the feet were still once more. Frank picked up the gun and tucked it into his belt.

TEN

The bunk-house was a rocking inferno of swirling gunsmoke, lit intermittently by flashes which revealed the forms crouching behind their fantastic barricades. Their smoke-grimed faces, their flashing eyes, and bared white teeth.

Another torch was thrown by the attackers. It thudded on the roof, rolled in a shower of sparks, and fell to the sod below; but another one was already on its way. This one hit the roof and stuck. The smell of wood-smoke began to filter into the bunk-house, to mingle with the gunsmoke that was like a fog around the beseiged party.

Kramer ran to the kitchen door. Big Bill Pretty turned. 'Get 'em movin',' he said.

Kramer ran back and began to grasp the shoulders of the cursing, firing men, and yell in their ears.

Half-crouching, they rose one by one, still firing.

Dobson said: 'How about ol' Cal? We cain't leave ol' Cal tuh be burnt.'

'We won't,' said Kramer. 'Give me a hand.'

They carried the blanket-shrouded body of Cal Bennett out to a horse and tied him on swiftly with a riata.

Everyone but Big Bill mounted. He had climbed back to his perch and was pouring lead from his two Colts, keeping the attackers at bay.

'C'mon, Bill,' yelled Kramer.

The giant emptied his Colts. Then he grabbed his rifle and ran for it. The bunch set off at a furious gallop. Behind them the roof of the bunk-house was beginning to crackle merrily. The attackers were still shooting.

The six men, with the horse carrying its still burden, galloping with them, turned their heads as they reached the crest of the rise. The bunk-house was a mass of flames now, and, fanned by the breeze, the fire was spreading to the other buildings.

In the ever-spreading glow, black figures were running around like large, scurrying ants. Then they bunched together and began to move out of the circle of fire.

'Here they come!' yelled Olly Masters. 'An' I bet they're plumb ravin'.'

Frank Carter took one last look back at the fiery pyre that had been the only home he ever knew, but there was no sadness in his heart; only that unalterable bitterness. He followed the others, and the flaming sight was blotted from his view.

Billy the Indian, who had hearing like a prairie-dog, heard the steady drumming of approaching hooves and rose from his cot. Moving gently, so as not to disturb his snoring squaw and the four bundled papooses, he put on his moccasins and his trousers. Then he took the old Sharps buffalo-gun from behind the head of the cot and stole from the little one-roomed cabin and into the night.

He ran noiselessly to the head of the narrow defile that was the only entrance to his little basin-home – unless you risked a terrible tumble by descending the steep, rocky slope at the back – and lay flat on his stomach behind a huge boulder. He nursed the heavy Sharps and waited as the horsemen came nearer.

They had reached the other end of the defile now. As they entered it and approached nearer the sheer stone walls of the tunnel-like place sent up fantastic echoes until it seemed there were hundreds of men and horses storming the place. But Billy, whose practised ears were accustomed to such trickery, could tell that there were only half a dozen or so horsemen in the band.

They were almost upon him now. He raised his head and shoved the muzzle of the buffalo-gun across the top of the rock.

Then a voice called: 'Billy! Are you there, Billy?'

'I am here, boss,' The Indian's deep voice boomed into the tunnel. He rose to his feet.

Next moment the horsemen were all around him. Trouble J boys, who were his mentors and friends. Naturally, although he knew things weren't all as they should be at the ranch – particularly since the death of Boss Bill – he was surprised to see them here, and in such an agitated state. With his sharp black eyes he noted three of them were wounded – counting the giant with the swaddled face – and he didn't need telling what the bundle was on the riderless horse.

Concisely, Kramer told him all he had to know. Billy grunted and nodded. He needed no orders, he was a man of deeds but very few words. He led them back to the cabin, where his squaw was already roused. She had plenty experience with wounded men.

Kramer said: 'I think we've shaken 'em off, but we gotta be sure. A couple of us 'ud better stand guard.'

'I'll go,' said Frank.

'I'll come with yuh,' said Dobson. 'An' Lafe can stay an' help the squaw with the wounded.'

'Durned lip,' said the foreman; but, knowing it was for the best, he stayed.

Billy saw to the horses. He carried the pitiful bundle that had been lashed to one of them and placed it in a safe cache behind the cabin.

Frank Carter and the monkey-faced Dobson walked back along the defile, their boot-heels echoing hollowly in the stillness. When they reached the other end, they climbed a little and took their stands behind a tall knob of rock.

Dobson produced the 'makings' and rolled himself a cigarette.

'Want one, Frank?'

The youth nodded, so Dobson rolled another one and handed it to him. Once more the fact of Frank's disability was brought home to him. As he lit the cigarette at the flaming match in the man's cupped hands, he realized that, had it been anybody else but him, Dobson would have handed them the 'makings' so they could 'help themselves.' But, with a damned crooked arm like he'd got, and only two pretty useless fingers on that hand, he could not roll a cigarette.

Frank was silent in his bitter thoughts, his shotgun between his legs as he squatted with his back against the rock, the cigarette dangling from his tight lips. Dobson was silent, too, a rifle across his knees. Probably he was thinking of his dead pard, Bennett.

The breeze whispered among the hills. Far away an animal howled – too far away to be sure what it was. The man and the youth sat and smoked.

When they had finished their cigarettes, they talked desultorily for a few moments, but nothing interested either of them, so they sank into silence once more. This still inactivity, after the blustering babble at the old Trouble J, was beginning to tell on them, hard-bitten though they were – even the kid, who, his companion reflected to himself, hardly seemed human at times since his dad was killed.

A rumbling in the distance that sounded like approaching horsemen enlivened them a bit, but it died down. If it had been the Judson mob, they had evidently gone off on a wrong track. Or maybe it was just thunder in the air, herald of an approaching storm. It was a warm, oppressive, silent night now. Their grimy clothes stuck to their bodies and little beads of sweat tickled their smoke-begrimed faces.

Footsteps echoed in the defile, and Lafe Kramer and Bill Pretty came to relieve them. The big man's head looked like a huge pudding with the new white cloth swathed around it.

Thankfully, the other two retraced their steps. They drank the scalding hot coffee Billy made for them and ate a few corn biscuits, then they dossed down with the others on the outside of the cabin.

Dawn was washing the sky with a dull, slatey-grey when Frank Carter awoke.

In the half-light he had breakfast with Kramer, Dobson, and Pretty. McDougal and Masters were up on the look-out. After Dobson and Frank had finished their hot beans, *tamales*, made as only Billy could, and boiled strip-pork, they went to relieve the two men.

As they looked out across the mesa it was being washed by a pale, watery light. The near horizon was burdened by a line of heavy, purplish clouds.

'Shore looks like a blow comin',' said Dobson.

Half an hour later they were relieved by Billy. They knew why, and their thoughts were grim as they returned along the defile. The first heavy drops of rain plummetted from the lowering sky and burst on the hard rock around them.

In a patch of soil beneath a small gnarled tree, Big Bill and Kramer were digging a grave. Masters and McDougal stood watching. The dark, blocky man had his hand so swathed in bandages that it looked like a fantastic white club. Lean, blond McDougal had his arm in a sling. At their feet, like a silent presence, was the bundle in the dark grey blanket. It had once been Cal Bennett. Dobson looked at it, then seized a spade from Big Bill and began to dig furiously.

They rolled the pitiful bundle into the trench and covered it up.

On a rude cross made from two thick slats nailed together, Dobson burnt an inscription with a hot iron:

CAL BENNETT. DIED JUNE 14, 18—

And beneath that, as a token, his own initials: J.D.

Dobson didn't know when Bennett was born, or anything like that. He only knew that he had met him in Tombstone about nine years ago. They had roamed together, punching cows all over the West. About six years ago they landed up at the Trouble J. They liked the country, and they liked Bill Carter, so they stayed there.

Dobson had heard Tombstone was a ghost-town now.

Mel Sterndale, editor of the *Georgetown Herald*, beamed as he drew the first proof from his machine. He held it up so that the shafts of late afternoon sunlight through the dusty window shone full on the damp printed sheet.

'Shorty!' he called.

A stocky younker with a good natured apple-face bobbed up from behind the piled drawers that held the type. He was still busy sorting out the mess Ralph Messiter and his strong-arm men had made the night before. Right behind where he crouched had lain the dead, blood-soaked body of Homer Larrabee. That fact gave Shorty a pleasurable thrill.

'Yeah, boss.'

'C'mon here, and have a look at this.'

Wiping his hands on his filthy jeans, Shorty joined his boss.

He read aloud the headlines on the printed sheet:

*SHOTGUN KID THUMBS NOSE AT KING
JUDSON AND HIS MERRY MEN.*

'Wow!' said Shorty. 'You're not gonna offer that fer sale on the streets, are yuh, boss?'

'What do I print the paper for?' said Sterndale. 'If they

won't buy 'em, I'll give 'em away. First thing I'm gonna
do is tack this up on the window where everybody can see
it. That ought to boost the demand some, I reckon.'

'I reckon,' said Shorty weakly, and went back to his post.
It was right near the back door, anyway.

Gee, things sure were popping in Georgetown lately.
There were four or five stiffs in Dry Dust Weeks's Funeral
Parlour since the ruckus last night at the Trouble J.

Shorty had no yen to join those stiffs. He tried to
concentrate on his work, but, despite himself, he had to
keep peeping at his boss, who was methodically pasting
the news-sheet on the window outside as if it were a harm-
less bill of sale or something.

He finished it and, wiping his hands in a satisfied way,
came back into the shop and started up the printing press
once more.

He was working away manfully, whistling to himself,
when a stone crashed through the window, narrowly miss-
ing his head.

He looked out. Two men stood in the middle of the
street. One of them threw another rock – a bigger one this
time. Sterndale dodged. The rock smashed into the
middle of the press and was jammed. The machinery
stopped with a whirring crash. One of the men leered at
Sterndale and patted his gun. Then they made off.

The editor turned back to the machine. Part of the type
in the form he had on the platen was smashed. The rock
had got caught and had stopped the machine. Sterndale
dislodged it with a type-mallet and started the machine
again. No damage done to that, anyway; but he'd have to
reset part of the type.

With infinite patience, he got the form out and placed
it on the table. He took out the battered type, and, joining
Shorty at the cases, began to set up some more.

'That was a coupla Judson men, wasn't it, boss?' said the
youth.

'Yes, I think it was.'

'I guess they were mighty het-up about thet poster. I guess they're off tuh tell their pals.'

'Maybe they are,' said Sterndale. 'Look, Shorty; if they come making a lotta trouble, you dodge out the back door and go tell Sheriff Budd.'

'Sure, boss. D'yuh think they'll come?'

'No, I don't think so, Shorty,' said the editor as he left the lad. 'But I don't want you tuh get mixed up in any arguments.'

He looked ruefully at the broken window. Still, he was used to that. If that was all they did, he wasn't worrying none.

He was bent over his press once more when, out of the tail of his eye, he saw Lye Spar stop outside the window. With him was the snake-eyed gambler, Ralph Messiter. He looked kind of dishevelled and tired.

Spar reached up a lean arm and tore a wide strip from the page on the window. Out of the corner of his other eye, Sterndale saw the back door close behind Shorty. Spar was still tearing away. When the window was stripped to his liking, he opened the door and came in. Messiter followed him, and, out of hiding, came other men. They filed in until the little printshop seemed full of them. Messiter was swinging a multi-looped riata in his hand.

It was he who spoke first. 'I'm back, Mr Sterndale.'

'So I see,' said the editor. 'And you've brought Mr Lye Spar with you,' He bowed ironically. 'I'm honoured.'

'Cut the cackle,' snarled Spar, who was of a different calibre to the suave gambler. 'We've come fer only one thing, Sterndale. That is tuh wipe your stinking newspaper office off the map an' run you out of Georgetown. The folks here've stood your cheek long enough. It's time you peddled your pretty speeches some place else—'

They all began to move nearer to the editor. Instinctively, he moved across in front of his press.

Suddenly Messiter moved in close and lashed out at him. Sterndale blocked the blow. He moved back against the press, and his hand grasped the type-mallet.

Messiter jumped back just in time, the heavy wooden implement whistled down past his aquiline nose.

'Get him,' snarled Spar.

The men moved in on all sides. Desperately, but without fear, Sterndale flailed around him with the mallet. One man went down stunned. Another staggered away, spitting blood. Then a gun-barrel crashed on Sterndale's shoulder, making him drop the weapon with a cry of pain. Fists beat him to his knees. He was dazed and bleeding as Messiter dropped the noose of the riata over his arms and pulled it tight.

Some of the men had moved away now and were carrying on systematically with their destruction.

Cursing them through puffed lips, Sterndale was hauled to his feet. It was then the deep voice spoke from the doorway.

'Let him go! Back up, all of yuh!'

It was Sheriff Joe Budd, and he had a levelled Colt in each of his huge fists. Watching the old man, whose bulk filled the doorway, the men around Sterndale began to move away from him, leaving him standing, swaying a little.

'Thanks, Sheriff,' he said.

The wreckers stood still, watching the guns and waiting 'You again, Spar,' said Joe Budd.

'Keep your nose outa this,' snarled the little gunnie.

A round, red face appeared round the corner of the window and a voice yelled: 'Look out, Sheriff.'

The old man turned, but he was not quick enough. The descending gun-barrel crumpled his hat. His knees sagged. One of the watchers kicked the guns from his hands.

Shorty's face vanished again, and he could be heard running along the boardwalk. Two more men appeared in the doorway behind the sheriff, who was on his knees now, shaking the leonine grey head like a wounded beast.

'You'll pay fer this, Spar,' he said.

'You're finished, Budd,' snarled the other. 'Take him an' lock him in one of his own cells. Hit him over the haid again if he starts actin' funny.'

The two men prodded Joe Budd forward with their guns. 'Get movin', Sheriff.' He began to move slowly along the boardwalk with them close behind him.

The editor of the *Georgetown Herald* was forced to look on while his beloved establishment was reduced to a shambles. The men smashed the machinery with hammers they had brought along for the purpose; they smashed the cases and drawers, and strewed the type underfoot. They tore paper into shreds, piled it in the middle of the floor, and tipped treacly black, green, and red ink in a sticky mess all over it.

Sterndale had quit wasting his breath in shouted invective. The rope cut cruelly into his arms. He was quiet, tight-lipped. Only his eyes blazed in his bruised and bloodied face.

More people clustered around the door and the windows to watch the fun. Even if they didn't hold with such rough work, they had to remain passive. They were outnumbered by Judson supporters and habitual hangers-on from the Curly Cat and other dives. Quieter and older folk looked in, wondered what had happened to the town's law and order and passed on.

'That's enough,' barked Lye Spar, and the wreckers ceased and stood back to admire their handiwork.

'Let's have him outside,' said the little gunman. 'Clear the way!'

The people faded away from the doorway, and Mel Sterndale was dragged outside. The riata was taken from around his body, and with a shorter piece of rope his hands were lashed behind his back.

A flea-bitten nag with rolling vacuous eyes was brought forward and, amid the ribald laughter of the onlookers, he was lashed to it, his legs fastened beneath its sagging belly, his head facing the beast's bony rump.

'Did yuh get the other tackle?' bawled Lye Spar.

'Yeah,' shouted another voice. 'We got it. Widder Biggs didn't like us havin' her feather bed, but we got it.'

Only then did Mel Sterndale realize the full measure of what was in store for him. Gales of cruel laughter swept through the crowd. They were a merciless mob now.

'Black him up, Conny!' yelled somebody.

Then a diversion occurred. The little round figure of Lawyer Herbert Markson came shooting through the ranks of the lookers-on. His little piggy face was flushed, his little piggy eyes gleaming with indignation.

'What's goin' on?' he shrilled. 'What are you doing?' Lye Spar turned around to face him. Very slowly, as if speaking to a child, he said: 'We're gonna tar an' feather Mr Sterndale an' run him out of town.'

'You can't do it! I won't let you! Where's the sheriff?'

'The sheriff's locked-up in his own jail.'

Markson began to splutter. 'You can't mess with the law – you can't do that – let that man free immediately—'

He broke off with a little gurgle as Spar's gun flashed into his hand.

The little gunman's eyes gleamed wickedly, his teeth showing in a little snarl.

'Shall I fill yuh full of holes to let some o' the air out of yuh?' As he advanced, the lawyer began to back away, holding his podgy hands in front of him as if to protect himself from physical blows.

'Don't shoot,' be spluttered. 'Don't shoot.'

Then he backed into the front ranks of the crowd and they caught hold of him. He was lifted into the air, and, squealing and struggling, passed over their heads. At the back, amid jeering laughter, they bounced him on the sidewalk. He scrambled to his feet and scuttled for the safety of his office. The crowd turned once more to the main event.

'Let him have it, Conny!'

'Trim him up nice an' pretty, Conny.'

Conny, a half-wit who helped out in the livery stables, winked and nodded and leered.

He put down his buckets and climbed on to the saddle of another horse that stood beside the one on which Sterndale was mounted. The little editor was quiet now, his bruised lips tightly compressed, his eyes hooded, but his head high as he sat on the ribbed bare back of the ancient nag and awaited his crowning humiliation.

The crowd became silent, rather with a subtle awe than any finer feeling, as Conny raised the first bucket.

ELEVEN

Milly La Moure stood at the window of her room in the Curly Cat. Her shapely form was clad in a purple silk dressing-gown; her blonde hair was loose, cascading over her shoulders. She was listening, her blue eyes wide, her smooth white forehead finely wrinkled. Her window was in the corner of the building, and the framework of the ornate false front prevented her from seeing much of the street below.

Her window was open to let in a breath of dry, dusty air. The din that floated up to her prevented her from hearing Mervyn Judson enter the room. She started violently as his arms slid around her waist.

'What's the matter, pet?' he said.

'Merv, what's the din? What's goin' on down the street?'

'The boys are teachin' Mel Sterndale a lesson. They're gonna run him outa town.'

'What for?'

'What for?' mimicked Judson harshly. 'You've read his latest news-sheets, ain't yuh?'

'Yeah – he only says what he thinks.'

'Wal, I don't like what he thinks. Lotsa people are gettin' fed-up of havin' what he thinks crammed down their throats. This mawnin' he'd got another cheeky bill posted up on his window. The town's given him too much rope—'

'By the town, I guess you mean you, Merv,' said Milly softly.

He stopped in the middle of his tirade and eyed her suspiciously. Ruthless egoist that he was, he sometimes found Milly hard to understand; but there was no shade of humour on her doll-like face.

He said: 'I put the town on the map, didn't I? An' all people like Sterndale've done is blame every cussed thing that happens on me an' my boys – I own Georgetown. I—'

He stopped. Milly was not listening. She was staring out of the window. After a quiet lull, the clamouring had started up again, nearer and more savage.

Then the beginning of the cavalcade moved into the strip of the main drag that lay beneath her gaze.

'Merv!' she burst out. 'What's this? Oh! They've tarred and feathered him. Oh, how cruel!'

She turned away from the pitiable sight and looked up into the face of the man behind her. His eyes were glowing strangely, there was a little smile on the lips beneath the bar of black moustache.

He said: 'He can think himself lucky he ain't goin' out on a shutter.'

'They're turnin' him out of town like that—' Milly shuddered as she had another glimpse of the fantastic figure on the tottering nag, the two of them like one feathered monstrosity. 'Out in the sun – if nobody finds him, he'll die. It's beastly – beastly! He's a good man. I've always liked him. You're doin' that to him because he said a few things about yuh – all of them true—'

She broke off with a sharp cry of pain as his hand gripped her wrist. He swung her away from the window to face him in the middle of the room.

'You'll hafta be careful what you say, my pet.'

'That's all I am,' gasped the girl. 'Your pet! Everybody in the town's gotta be your pet if they want to stay healthy. You're mad – you an' all your men – mad!'

He drew his arm back and lashed her across the mouth with the back of his hand. She tumbled into the corner of the room and lay sobbing hysterically. He stormed out, banging the door behind him with such force that it rattled the open window. The cries of the mob were fainter now.

For a moment she lay as she had fallen, then rose and looked at her bruised, tear-stained face in the mirror. For a moment, it looked ugly and old as she cursed the fate that had brought her to the life she led. A life that at first had excited her with its colour and change, but of late was becoming bitter and terrifying. Emotions chased each other across her face as she looked at herself in the mirror and also, for the first time in many years, looked into her own soul. What she saw there was not good. But maybe there was still hope!

She ran to the window as feet tramped below. The mob, now a more subdued muttering mass, was returning. She heard the heavy boot-heels as they marched into the saloon below, and their brave cries as they congratulated each other. She sat down in a chair and began to pluck nervously at the silk of her dressing-gown. She loved nice things.

She ran her tongue around her swollen lips. Her eyes were frightened and uncertain. She struggled with her thoughts. Finally, she came to a decision and rose purposefully. She took off her dressing-gown and began to array herself in her riding clothes.

She omitted to give her last look into the glass to see if everything was to her liking. She crossed to the door, opened it and looked out.

Down below, the clamour was intensified, but up here all was quiet. She knew the girls would be down there whooping up the customers. Ordinary times she knew Judson would have wanted her there, too. She had to take the risk of him coming for her.

She went down the back stairs and got her pony from the little private stables, used solely by Curly Cat employees. She left the town by the back way, too, and pretty soon was out on the trail.

Oakie Budd was washing dishes for Mrs Lopez, the half-breed woman who cooked and dusted for the sheriff. He heard the clamour from down the street, but did not attach a lot of importance to it. Georgetown was getting a mighty rowdy place of late.

But he started and almost dropped a dish he was drying when somebody hammered on the back door and a voice shouted: 'Oak! Oak!'

He opened it. It was his friend, Shorty, the printer's apprentice. He was panting, his hair stood on end, his eyes started from his head.

'Oak,' he gasped. 'Your dad – in the jail – Sterndale – tarred and feathered.'

'Dad in the jail. Who? What are you talkin' about?'

'I tell yuh!' Shorty was getting his voice back and he was kind of het-up. 'Judson's men smashed up the printshop – they've tarred and feathered Mr Sterndale. When your dad tried tuh stop 'em they hit him over the head – then they took him an' locked him in his own jail—'

'Wait,' said Oak, and left him.

When he returned he was tucking a Colt .45 into his belt.

'Come on,' he said.

'Not me,' said Shorty. 'All I wanted tuh do wuz tell yuh. They've got it in fer me already. I don't wanna be tarred an' feathered.' He scuttled off.

Young Oakland, like his father, had a Herculean frame. Also, like his father, he had a fiery temper; but, as yet, unbridled by age and discretion. As he strode down main street he was boiling.

He did not heed the cautionary broken English of Mrs Lopez that floated after him.

His boot-heels thudded outside the door of the sheriff's office. His hand was on his gun as he flung the door open.

'All right, kid,' said one of the two men inside. 'Keep your hands out. Come in an' close the door.'

Oak looked into the barrel of the levelled Colt. He kicked the door to behind him with his heel.

'Where's my dad?' he said.

'He's nice and cosy,' said the narrow-faced gunman. His companion, a pock-marked 'breed, nursed his Colt on his knee and watched, with black beady eyes that reminded Oak of a diamond-backed rattler.

'Sit down, son,' said the narrow-faced one. 'Make yourself at home.'

Watching the man warily, Oak perched himself on the edge of the desk. His wrath had subsided; he felt cold inside, but he wasn't scared.

He said: 'You're buckin' the law now. Yuh won't get away with it.'

Still silent, the 'breed got up from the bench, crossed to the youth, and jerked the gun from his belt.

'Sassy young cuss, ain't he?' said narrow-face. 'Takes after his paw.'

As the 'breed turned away, Oak hit him on the side of the neck, knocking him against his companion. Then he dived. Narrow-face's gun went off. The slug ploughed a hole in the roof. Then the gun was knocked from his hand. The 'breed rolled away and landed on his hands and knees, his face against the bench. His companion tried to rise and was knocked back by Oak's large, meaty fist flush in his teeth.

The 'breed turned, trying to bring his gun up. Oak's long arm swung round, his fist smacked into the side of the 'breed's head. Oak grabbed for the gun as the man let it go. He heard his dad yelling back in the cells, then the front door crashed open and a voice barked:

'Drop that gun, younker.'

Oak stiffened; cold prickles went up and down his back. He let the gun slide from his hand. It hit the boards with a dull thud. He turned to face Mervyn Judson, Lye Spar, Ralph Messiter. They all had guns in their hands.

Judson began to laugh as his dishevelled, disgruntled gun-guards clambered to their feet.

'I thought I told you boys to treat the law gently,' he said. 'Haw! Haw! Fine hard cases I got – lettin' a kid rough 'em around.'

The narrow-faced gunnie looked sheepish. The 'breed was murderous, and the look he shot at the stalwart young man was token that he would not forget this humiliation in a hurry.

'Where's the ol' man?' said Judson.

'In the cells, boss.'

'Pick up your guns and get him out then. Careful – mind the younker don't jump again. Haw! Haw!'

Spar and Messiter joined in their chief's jeering laughter as the two hard cases went into the cell-block to fetch Joe Budd.

A few minutes later they ushered the cursing sheriff into the office. He stopped dead.

'Oak,' he ejaculated. 'What've the skunks done tuh you?'

'They ain't done anythin' tuh me, Dad,' said the young man with a faint smile.

Judson began to guffaw again. The sheriff took a step forward. The saloon-owner jerked his gun meaningly.

'Sit down, Joe.'

The old man's grey eyes blazed, his lined face was taut. Slowly, he went round behind his desk and sat down in his chair.

'You hold all the aces now, Judson,' he said. 'But it won't last. Your sort never do. I won't rest until you an' all your mob are run out of Georgetown.'

'Pity you feel like that, Joe,' said the poker-faced man suavely. 'I wuz figurin' maybe we could get together.'

'I'd sooner get together with a lobo wolf.'

'If you won't play along, things are gonna be a little onesided, Joe.'

'My time'll come.'

Judson stuck his face forward a little. For a moment the mask dropped. Murder gleamed in his eyes.

'I could break you right now.'

'Go ahead. You know you wouldn't get away with it. The law 'ud get yuh in the end.'

'I am the law here,' said Judson, his voice and features composed again. 'An' the sooner you realize it the better it'll be for you—'

'I'll never realize it. I'm still Sheriff o' Georgetown. Right now, what I want to know is what've yuh done with Mel Sterndale?'

'The boys run him outa town.'

'Run him outa town?'

'You heard what the boss said,' snarled Lye Spar stepping forward, his gun poised. 'Let me slash him one, Merv, an' be finished with it. The ol' jackass gets in my craw.'

'Hold your hosses, Lye,' said Judson. 'Don't let y'self be bothered by a silly ol' man. Come on, we'll get going. Though what I really came for, Sheriff, was to apologize for any inconvenience my men have caused you. Although a good Western lawman should know when not to stick his nose intuh things. Like I told yuh before, Joe, you're ridin' for a fall – an ol' man like you shouldn't go rumpagin' around at full gallop. One o' these days it's gonna cost you your neck—'

The sheriff rose to his feet, his hands groping where his guns should be, his eyes flaming with impotent fury.

'Are you threatening me?'

Judson shook his head gently as he shepherded his men

from the office. 'It's a good job we took your guns from you. You're liable to shoot somebody.'

Joe Budd sat back in his chair, his wrath subsiding suddenly. 'My time'll come,' he said softly as the door closed behind the five men.

He rose and went just inside the door of the cell-block. 'Plenty o' guns in the armoury cupboard,' he said as he took the key from his vest pocket.

When he returned he had a new gun in each of his low-slung holsters. He handed another one to Oak.

'Stick that in your belt,' he said gruffly.

Father and son looked at each other – and understood. Oak was no longer a boy.

'What yuh gonna do, Dad?' he said.

'Nothin' at all at present, son,' said the sheriff. 'Caution – I've still gotta learn tuh keep my temper – an' I should advise you to do the same. First of all, we gotta find out who's with us.' Then his voice sobered as he added: 'Though I'm afeard there ain't a 'ull lot of 'em, Oak.'

Milly La Moure caught up with the crazy, bobbing monstrosity that was Mel Sterndale and his nag, well past the sandstone buttes. Maddened with fear, the old horse had galloped erratically until it was utterly spent and could only wobble along at a walking pace. The man tied to its back was sagged forward on its flea-bitten mane and was tossed about with every awkward movement.

As the sun beat down, steam was rising from the sticky mess that entirely covered the man – and a lot of the horse's body, too: melted tar was still dripping from its trembling flanks.

Milly took a small clasp-knife from her saddle-bag and, getting her hands and sleeves bedaubed with the stuff, cut the man's hands, then his legs free. Sterndale swayed. She dismounted from her horse and held on to him. She helped him to slide to the ground and then, disregarding the damage to her natty riding outfit, helped him to the softer ground beside the trail. There his weight proved too much for her and she let him go. He slumped into a half-sitting, half-reclining position. She clasped her hands together impotently as she bent over him. Through the tar that gummed up his features he tried to mumble his gratitude.

She ran back to her horse and wrenched free her small blanket. With this she tried to mop away some of the evil-smelling, feather-bedaubed muck with which the man was entirely covered. What could she do for him? Where could she take him? She could have cursed at her own helplessness. Then, looking up, she saw the two horsemen approaching.

For a moment panic numbed her senses and turned her legs to jelly. Then she realized there was a ten-to-one chance against the riders being Judson men – particularly coming from that direction. She took a chance, and, standing erect, waved. They did not wave back, but came on steadily.

She became scared again, but it was too late to run now. She could only stand and wait. She raised her hand to her forehead to shade her eyes from the sun-glare.

She did not know whether to be scared or relieved when she recognized the riders as Lafe Kramer and the young cripple, Frank Carter.

Kramer dismounted. 'Good gosh,' he said. 'Who is it?'

The girl's reply came in a rush. 'It's Mel Sterndale. They run him outa town like that. Merv's boys. I – I couldn't see him go like that, I had to come out to see if I could help him. Oh, I'm glad somebody's come. If only you can do something.'

The cold grey eyes in the lean predatory face seemed to bore into her.

'I – I'm not as bad as the rest of them. I couldn't see him go like that. Will you help me?'

She looked at the thin kid with the crooked arm who

still sat his horse. Was this the Frank Carter she remembered? In the pinched face and blue eyes there was only ruthlessness. She looked back at the big man. It seemed to her that his face had softened a little.

He said: 'We'll look after him, Miss Milly.' He went down on his knees beside Sterndale.

The little editor was rousing and had managed to wipe some of the muck from his face.

'It's good tuh see yuh, Lafe,' he croaked.

The big man fetched his water-canteen, an item that Milly in her haste had forgotten to bring. Sterndale took a deep, grateful swig. Then with Kramer's help, he got to his feet.

'Let's wrap the blanket right around yuh, ol'-timer, like you wuz an Injun papoose,' said Kramer.

He and the girl did this, then helped the little printer to mount Kramer's horse. The latter mounted up behind him.

From his perch, cruel and alien in his disability, unable to help because of it, Frank Carter watched the whole proceedings without speaking.

Her natty riding habit crumpled and bedaubed, her hands and her face black, Milly La Moure walked slowly towards her pony. Then she turned suddenly, looking up into the face of the big man.

'Take me with yuh, Mr Kramer,' she said.

For a moment the hard lines seemed to soften again, the grey eyes reveal a flicker of warmth. Then the man said:

'We cain't do that, Miss Milly. Where we're goin' there's no place for a woman. Ef'n you'll take my advice you'll go back to Georgetown, get your duds together, an' get out of there as quick as you can.'

Sbe tried not to reveal the cold fear that clutched at her heart. 'I'll do that, Mr Kramer,' she said. She mounted her horse.

'Let's get goin',' said Frank Carter harshly.

When the girl looked back they were bobbing shapes like blobs of dust, rapidly receding in the heat-haze. She felt like turning her horse and following them, but she pressed on to Georgetown.

Kramer and Frank made tracks for the hills that nursed Billy the Indian's home. That little, naturally fortified basin was, for the time being, their hide-out.

Taking a risk, they had been reconnoitring around the blackened ruins of the Trouble J. Although he did not show it, Frank was glad to discover his pa's grave was untouched. Coming away from there, they had spotted those bobbing specks on the trail, had seen one overtake the other, and the get-together that ensued. They figured it needed investigating.

Mel Sterndale was mighty thankful and grateful for the hornery curiosity that had brought them to his side. He felt fit to talk now; the treatment he had received had far from broken his spirit. He began to tell his story as they rode.

TWELVE

Milly arrived at the Curly Cat, left her pony in the stables, and crept up the back stairs. Downstairs the clamour was louder than ever, and she heard a sound that froze the blood in her veins.

They were chanting: 'We want Milly! We want Milly!' She ran along the deserted landing and opened the door of her room. Then she gave a gasp, her clenched fist going to her mouth in a horrified gesture. Sitting in the armchair by the window was Mervyn Judson.

'Hullo, my pet,' he said. 'Come in, an' shut the door behind you.'

Numbly, she obeyed him. Then she stood uncertain, her blue eyes wide, like a weasel hypnotized by a snake.

'My, you are in a pickle,' he said. 'So you found our friend Sterndale. What did you do with him?'

She found her voice – and a measure of courage. 'He's where you can't find him.'

'Like that, is it?' said Judson softly. He shrugged his shoulders. 'Wal, we won't argue about it now. Get dressed – you're wanted downstairs.'

The girl did not speak. Her face was deathly white and drawn. She crossed the room, and from a corner produced a battered suitcase. She opened this on the bed and then went to her wardrobe.

'What's the idea?' snarled Judson.

'I'm leaving.'

His eyes blazed. He rose from the chair and crossed the room in one bound. He caught hold of her arm and twisted it cruelly behind her back. She cried out with pain.

'What the hell's got into yuh?' he snarled. 'You'll stay here an' do yuh job – an' like it. Get them fancy duds on an' get downstairs.'

'I won't,' panted the girl.

He exerted more pressure. Beads of sweat stood on her white forehead. She moaned.

He threw her from him. She sprawled on the floor. With a quick movement, he unbuckled his ornate leather belt and swished it in the air. The girl cowered.

He swung the belt so that the cruel steel buckle glinted in the sunshine.

'I oughta kill you,' he hissed. 'You damned Jezebel.' He slashed the belt within an inch of her face. She cried out in terror.

He said: 'Are yuh gonna carry on, or do I hafta stop yuh altogether?' His meaning was plain. The girl cringed. She nodded her head.

'Good,' he said. 'Now while you're in the mood, you can tell me what happened with Sterndale.'

She shook her head. 'You won't find him.'

He swished the belt again. 'I don't want to mark yuh, Milly, it'd be bad business. But, by hell—'

'I'll tell yuh,' she said dully, and told him all the circumstances of the little editor's rescue.

'You bitch,' he said. 'I oughta cut yuh to ribbons. It's a good job you're of use tuh me – clean yourself up an' get your flashiest duds on. Let's see yuh downstairs pronto. An' don't try tuh make a run for it – unless you want to be tarred an' feathered, too.'

The girl was beaten. She nodded her head dully as she got to her feet. Judson banged from the room. She heard him calling for Lye Spar.

A few moments later she heard a clattering of hooves in the street, and looked out. A bunch of horsemen were setting out with Judson and Spar at their head. She fervently hoped they would not catch up with Sterndale and his two rescuers. She remembered the lean, mahogany face of Lafe Kramer, the hard, grey eyes that could soften sometimes. A strange feeling filled her heart, choking her with tears that would not fall.

She knew that although Judson was gone he was sure to have put men to watch her. She finished dressing and went downstairs, to be greeted by the whistles and cheers of the customers.

Meanwhile, the Judson hellions, the pick of his gunfighting crew, were pushing their mounts to the utmost.

There were no signs of other riders on the seemingly limitless mesa. The horizon trembled in the heat-haze. Peering ahead, the men had to shade their eyes to protect them from the glaring sun.

'They've got too big a start,' said Spar. 'I guess they must've made for the hills.'

After another half-hour's hard riding, they left the grasslands behind and began to climb over sunbaked soil and rock. From his cunningly hidden perch, Frank Carter saw them. He raised his gun, ready to give the alarm if they came too near to the gang's natural hiding-place. He looked back to the defile, cunningly concealed by trailing shrubbery, and the cool basin beyond. There was no tell-tale smoke.

The searchers passed so close that he recognized the leaders easily. He smiled thinly as they meandered onwards. Kramer came along the defile to relieve him and was surprised when he heard the news.

He said: 'They must've got somethin' outa that girl an' come after us. I hope they haven't harmed the kid – she took a big chance. If she hadn't, Sterndale might've wandered around in that condition until he died. He'll be all right now. He's stripped an' bathin' himself in the stream. He ain't burned at all, but it's a helluva job to get the stuff off.'

Frank was silent for a few moments. Then he said: 'I'm figurin' it's time we had a crack at Judson. He's had his own way too long.'

'That's a bright thought, anyway,' said Kramer. He, too, was tired of inactivity; and, particularly since the rescue of Sterndale, raring to go and attempt to pay back some of the score that was rapidly mounting against the uncrowned king of Georgetown. Sterndale had told them of Judson's treatment of the sheriff: it was obvious what the big saloon-cum-ranchowner intended to be sole dictator of that territory.

Frank said: 'Why not tonight, Lafe? It'll be dark when that gang get's back. They'll be tired an' hornery, never expectin' us to strike back at 'em. Let us raid the Curly Cat—'

'You're a bloodthirsty young cuss,' said Kramer. 'But yuh got somethin'. If we take 'em by surprise – do all we can – then light out again— But it's a big risk. I guess we'll have the boys vote on it. I'd like tuh know what they've done tuh that gel,' he added slowly.

'Why not go back an' put it tuh the boys?' said Frank. 'I'll hang on here a mite longer an' keep my eyes peeled in case that gang pass this way again. Then we'll give 'em a start – we don't want to meet up with 'em on the trail or we'll be sunk.' He seemed to take it for granted that the rest of the boys would fall in with his plans.

They did not disappoint him, for, some time later, as twilight was falling, Kramer returned with the news that they were all raring to go.

Judson and his merry men arrived back in Georgetown – weary, hungry, travel-stained, and, to a man, mighty disgruntled. The big leader was very silent, his face like a thunder-cloud. His *segunda*, Lye Spar, was spitting like a sidewinder with his rattle caught in a bunch of cacti.

The mob packed into the Curly Cat, which was already pretty full, yelling for eats – and plenty of liquor to wash 'em down with. They began to drown their frustrations in redeye.

The chorus were giving an impromptu show on the little stage: Judson looked around for Milly but could not see her anywhere. His eyes narrowed, his lips curled beneath the heavy moustache. He looked murderous. He blamed all his disappointment and chagrin on the girl.

He went over to the bar and spoke to one of the white-aproned bartenders.

'Where's Miss Milly?'

'She went upstairs some time ago, boss.'

'All right. Bring me some eats an' some o' the best whiskey up tuh my room, will yuh?'

'Sure, boss.'

Judson stamped upstairs. He tried the door of the girl's room. It was locked.

'Milly!' he shouted. There was no answer. 'D'yuh want me tuh kick the damn' door in?' he bawled.

'All right,' said a weary voice from inside.

He heard the key click, then the door was opened.

Milly stood there, a glittering picture in her best gown, but her blonde hair was a little dishevelled, and she looked deadly tired.

He pushed past her into the room.

'Can't I ever have any privacy or rest?' she said. 'I said I'd stay, didn't I? Ain't that good enough for yuh? Yuh don't think I'd try to get away, do yuh, with six of your pet gunmen watchin' me?'

'Why aren't yuh downstairs amusin' the customers?' he said. 'Thet chorus are mumblin' around like a lot of spavined old cows.'

She kept the door open and held on to it. 'I'm tired,'

she said. 'I ain't used to bein' pushed around—'

'Don't tell me,' he jeered. 'You're on velvet here. All you're asked tuh do is a bit of singin'. Get yourself fresh-ened up – yuh look like a mangy bobcat right now – an' get downstairs again.'

'I suppose you didn't catch up with Sterndale an' the others,' she said. 'An' you've come back to take it outa me.'

He made for her, his fist raised, his face suffused with passion. She flinched. He dropped his hand.

'You won't look nice if I muss you around,' he said.

'I'm glad yuh didn't catch 'em,' she said. 'Glad.'

It was as if she was trying to goad him into destroying her. Her face was puffy, full of rage and misery. But now he only watched her with a sneer on his lips. A man came along the passage carrying his meal on a tray.

He said: 'I'm gonna eat now. You'd better be out of here when I come back.'

He walked past her and slammed the door in her face. When he returned, the door was locked again. He was uncertain whether she was in there or not. He called. There was no answer. Probably she had locked it behind her as she went. He clattered down the stairs. The stage was empty now. He could not see Milly. He asked for her. None of the barmen had seen her come downstairs. There was murder in his eyes as he retraced his steps.

He kicked the door of the girl's room. 'Milly!' he bawled. 'Open up!'

Still there was no answer. He threw all his weight against the door. It squealed protestingly, then gave way alto-gether. He staggered into the room.

The girl was sitting by the window. She seemed to be listening. She whirled, her face chalk-white.

'I'll teach you!' he snarled, and sprang for her.

Instinctively, she dodged. He blundered into the half-open window. It was then he heard the hoofbeats. They were close: they seemed to be entering the main drag and coming fast.

He leaned out of the window. Then he saw them coming down the street, passing like speeding phantoms across the bars of light that slashed it. He recognized them immediately and whipped out his gun. In a moment the girl was beside him.

'Look out,' she screamed. 'Here. Up—'

Then the slashing gun-barrel crashed on her head and she slumped to the floor. But her cries had been heard. The big man at the head of the column whipped out a gun and fired. Just in time, Judson dodged out of sight. The slug smashed the window in line where his head had been.

Down below they heard the shooting and the madly galloping hooves, and an apprehensive movement was made for the door.

The batwings crashed open and a horse came in, its big rider crouched low over its neck. He had a gun in each hand. One of them was already smoking.

'Lafe Kramer!' said somebody.

Behind him, on a paint pony, came young Frank Carter, his shotgun levelled. People in the saloon woke from their daze. Two of the bartenders drew guns.

Both the big man's Colts bucked and crashed in his hands. One barman gave a strangled scream and seemed as if he was trying to leap over the bar. He remained draped across it like a huge, sprawling doll. Blood gushed from his mouth and dyed the floor. His companion simply groaned and crumpled up out of his sight.

People cringed in panic from the horses' hooves. The two riders were side by side. Frank Carter's shotgun boomed. A big man near the bar who had reached for his gun had half his face blown away by a charge that shattered a mirror behind him and fetched down a shelf of glasses and bottles.

'Everybody up with their hands,' yelled Kramer. Other

ex-Trouble J men were filing into the saloon on foot. They all had a couple of guns apiece, out and levelled.

Hands began to go up. Even Lye Spar, who, since his meal, had been drinking at the bar, looked alarmed and raised his.

Merv Judson's face appeared round the top of the stairs. The gun in his hand spoke, but, as he was dodging, his aim was bad. The slug tipped Kramer's hat. Frank Carter's gun boomed. Only just in time was Judson's head out of sight. The hail of shot brought a shower of plaster from the ceiling.

Coolly, Frank began to reload. Kramer leapt from his horse.

'You know what tuh do, boys,' he said. 'I'm goin' after that skunk.'

He took the stairs two at a time, his twin guns held in front of him. He pulled up dead at the top before he poked the wide brim of his Stetson around the corner. In the gloom of the landing Judson's gun flamed. It boomed deafeningly. Kramer felt the breath of the slug as it ricochetted from the corner and whined until it was embedded in the ceiling, bringing another shower of plaster. The gun spoke again. This time the slug thumped harmlessly into the wall. Then Kramer heard boot-heels thudding, diminishing.

Taking a chance, he went round the corner, taking it wide, flattening himself against the opposite wall. Simultaneously, both men fired. A slug plucked at Kramer's sleeve. He thought he heard the other man gasp. Boot-heels thudded again. Through the blue haze of gunsmoke, Kramer saw the moving figure. He fired a split-second too late as it vanished. The boot-heels clattered now. *Back-stairs* flashed into Kramer's mind. He began to run.

As he passed a room, he had a confused impression of hearing frightened squeals. The chorus girls were hiding out. He pulled himself up short at the corner. A draught of cold air whipped up the stairs and down the passage.

Then a door banged. But maybe it was only a trick. Swiftly, Kramer stuck his Colt round the corner and pressed the trigger. There was no comeback: he followed with his body. The door at the bottom of the stairs was shut. He took the steps two at a time, almost slipping flat on his back at the bottom.

Hooves clattered outside. He flung open the door, then threw himself flat. Gunfire deafened him, slugs whined over his head. The hoofbeats thudded in a steady rhythm. He raised himself on his elbow and fired at the moving shape in the darkness. The hoofbeats began to fade. Cursing, he rose to his feet.

Judson was running out on the Curly Cat boys. Making for his ranch, no doubt. It was too late to get a horse and follow him now. Anyway, Kramer reflected, his place was with the boys.

As he ran back, he heard more shots down below, and began to get worried.

He was running down the passage when a woman ran out of the room. At first he did not recognize Milly.

There was blood on her forehead, and her blue eyes looked wild. They were also brimming with tears.

'Kramer,' she said imploringly. 'Don't leave me here. Take me with you.'

He remembered how she had called from the window, how she had saved Sterndale. No, he couldn't leave her here.

'C'mon,' he said gruffly. 'Keep behind me.'

The tears brimmed over and streamed down her cheeks as she followed him.

Kramer held out a cautionary hand as they got to the top of the stairs. He looked around the corner. Everything was under control down there. He beckoned her on.

The boys were relieving everybody of their guns, emptying the shells from them and tossing both guns and shells at random through the windows. They hadn't bothered to open them before they started. There was glass all over the place.

A man sat in a chair, moaning and nursing an arm that streamed with blood. Lye Spar was backed up against the bar; both his guns lay at his feet.

'Kick 'em over here, Lye,' said Olly Masters.

'Damn you,' said the gunman. But he booted the guns across to the dark, blocky cowboy.

Kramer's voice lashed the air. 'You kin have them back in a minute, Lye, an' we'll finish where we left off the other night.'

Spar's lips curled in a sneer that was a broad token of what he thought, but he did not speak again.

Jim McDougal was standing guard outside the saloon. He had only one arm in use, the other was still crooked into a white sling.

He stood in the shadows of the alley beside the saloon. From there he could watch the street but was unseen himself. Heads poked from doorways, but nobody had ventured further as yet.

Then McDougal saw the wide, easily recognized figure of Joe Budd striding down the street. With him was another big fellah. As they crossed a pool of light that spilled from a window, McDougal recognized Oak, the sheriff's son. He drew further back into the shadows.

The two men passed without seeing him. He admired their fearlessness as they approached the doors of the saloon. He stepped out and up behind them.

'Reach!' he said.

They froze in their tracks. 'Reach, I said!' Slowly, their hands went up. 'Now start walking again.'

As they carried on, wobbling on their high-heeled riding boots, their arms raised ludicrously in the air, McDougal shouted:

'I'm comin' in, boys! I've got a couple of visitors for you!'

He propelled the sheriff and his son into the saloon. Immediately, Dobson stepped forward and whipped their irons from their holsters.

The sheriff gave a shocked exclamation as he looked around him; the two horses, one of them without a rider, the other bearing the frail figure of Frank Carter and his inevitable shotgun; the dead bartender draped across the bar, his blood still dripping on the boards; the man with the shattered arm, who had fainted across a table; the unarmed Lye Spar against the bar; the broken glass that seemed to be all over the place; the Curly Cat habituees, their fangs drawn, piled up in two separate bunches – one in each corner – Kramer, a gun in each hand, a sardonic look on his face, beside him a rather bedraggled Milly; the pinched white face of the shotgun kid, with his strange blue eyes, leering down at him.

Jim McDougal went back into the street. There was another bunch of men approaching. He recognized the foremost one immediately. It was Ralph Messiter. The gambler saw him and went for his guns, dropping on one knee as he did so. McDougal fired but knew he had missed. Flame spurted from the kneeling man. Dodging behind a hitching-post, very inadequate cover, McDougal felt the wind of the slug.

The bunch was splitting up now. There were about ten of them. Other people, emboldened, were coming out of doors behind them. McDougal realized the boys would be hopelessly outnumbered. If they didn't get out now they'd be trapped. The men were trying to flank him. They fired as they came on. Some of the bullets came perilously close. He left his cover and dived for the batwings. Something that felt like a huge red-hot fist smote him in the back and propelled him into the saloon.

He tried to shout but could only manage a croak. His pard, Olly Masters, caught him as he tottered.

Lafe Kramer leapt into the saddle of his horse and

spurred him through the batwings. Frank Carter followed on his paint.

Kramer's gun blazed. The mob on the street broke in all directions. A hail of smallshot from Frank's sawn-off shotgun made them seek cover more quickly. Two luckless ones writhed in the middle of the street.

The rest of the Trouble J gang were running from the saloon now and forking their horses. Olly Masters helped McDougal to get into the saddle.

'Git goin'!' yelled Kramer above the din of gunfire. Then his own Colts began to speak again; he turned in the saddle, blazing away as the whole gang of them sped down the street in a ragged formation. A rider on a pony came out of the alley that led to the Curly Cat private stables and joined up with them. Turning his head, Lafe Kramer saw that Milly La Moure was riding beside him, her gown billowing, her head bare, her golden hair flying in the breeze.

The bullets of the other side now fell harmlessly short.

'We've got a start,' panted Kramer. 'They've gotta get their horses. An' their guns – a good many of them.' Then he saved his breath and his energy to push his mount to its utmost. Then they were out on the wind-blown range, a tight knot of them, riding hard.

THIRTEEN

Back in Georgetown, hooves clattered on the hard street as the first bunch of pursuers, led by the sheriff, his son, and Lye Spar, got under way. Maybe it gave the little gunman, malicious amusement to be riding with the law he despised.

Out on the range, Jim McDougal tumbled from his horse. The others slowed down at a shout from Olly Masters as the stocky man sprang from his horse and ran to his fallen pard.

'Gosh, Jim,' he said. 'I didn't know it wuz that bad. Why didn't yuh say?'

McDougal did not reply. His eyes were closed and he was breathing heavily. Big Bill Pretty ran to help.

'He'll have tuh come up with me,' said Masters. 'We ain't heavyweights like you; my hoss'll stand us.'

As they lifted McDougal up their hands got covered with blood from the wound in his back. They could hear the steady thrumming of their pursuers' horses now, coming nearer every second.

Masters held McDougal in the saddle.

'Easy does it, pard,' he said.

McDougal groaned as they began to gallop once more. Masters dropped into the van, shouting to the others that if they could go any faster to leave him.

141

Maybe he could keep just ahead, he thought, and they could cover him from the shelter of the little hide-out.

When the gang did reach Billy the Indian's little basin in the hills, the pursuers were almost in shooting distance.

The Trouble J boys dismounted, shoved their horses on out of range and sought the cover they knew so well.

'Now come on, you skunks!' said Big Bill Pretty.

Masters slid his pard gently from the saddle and into a soft patch at the base of a boulder.

'Now we'll soon have you fixed up, pard,' he said. 'Let me—' He paused, leaning closer, reaching forward with a hand to the still figure.

'Jim,' he said.

But McDougal was dead.

Masters wasted no time in lamenting. His was the first shot that tumbled a man from his horse. The posse halted and broke for cover then, as a fusillade greeted them.

Only Sheriff Budd came on like a man possessed. The firing died down. Then Frank Carter's shotgun boomed. The rider toppled from the saddle.

'You've hit the sheriff,' said Kramer.

'It's a pity,' said Frank tonelessly.

The burly figure of Oakland Budd ran from cover and began to drag his father away. Frank Carter raised the shotgun again. Then, slowly, he let the muzzle drop. Father and son disappeared into the shadows.

The posse opened up. They outnumbered the others, but they were in poor cover. Many of them just crouched in the long grass, hidden in the shadows, but the spurts of flame from their guns gave their positions away and allowed such a marksman as Big Bill Pretty to pick them off like sitting ducks. And Big Bill had no scruples or mercy; this was a battle, and he aimed to kill as many of the skunks as he could. He figured they had brought it on themselves. Kramer also squeezed the trigger deliberately and shot to kill. He knew that now the sheriff and his son had gotten into cover, all the rest of them were Judson men. The sheriff, with his mania for duty, had stuck his neck out once too often. Kramer cursed him for a crazy old fool – and yet was kind of sorry, too: he hoped the old-timer wasn't hit too bad, though he knew what a devastating weapon the younker's shotgun had proved to be.

His thoughts began to get balled up a little as the suddenly realized that, like a wraith, Milly La Moure was beside him once more, and handling a Winchester repeater as if she'd been born with it. The gel was certainly hard to figure. Anyway, he reckoned he didn't despise her now like he used to.

No amount of thinking could wholly impair his cold efficiency as a fighting machine. He squeezed the trigger mechanically and watched with satisfaction a figure rise to its knees with a gurgling scream, then crumple into the shadows once more. He swung his rifle and fired at another flash, but did not know whether he had hit anything this time.

One by one, the posse were being whittled mercilessly down. Out in the open like that, with very little cover, they did not stand much chance. They began to break and, still harried by fire, to run for their horses.

Suddenly, an agonized voice rang out. The young, vibrating voice of Oakland Budd.

'You've killed my father, Frank Carter. I'll get you if it's the last thing I do.'

Then, in a straggling bunch, the posse turned tail and ran. 'We cain't stay here,' said Lafe Kramer. 'There'll be a bigger bunch comin' from town. They'll know where to find us now. We've gotta get deeper into the hills. We ain't finished with Judson and his bunch yet.'

'You bet we ain't,' said Frank Carter.

The following morning, at dawn, when two large posses – one from the Cross M Ranch, the other from Georgetown, converged on the little hide-out in the hills, they discovered the birds had flown. They found the defile and advanced cautiously through it. The cabin in the hollow looked dead; no smoke came from its squat chimney; nothing was left inside except a few sticks of homemade furniture and a pile of cold ashes in the bricked grate. It was a squalid, dimly lit hole. They did not know with what reluctance Billy the Indian and his family had left it behind. They found the crudely marked grave of Cal Bennett, and gloated over the fact that they had depleted the ranks of the desperate gang by at least one.

'I think that McDougal got it, too,' said Ralph Messiter. 'They must've taken his body with 'em 'cos they were in such a hurry.'

Merv Judson made calculations. 'That leaves half a dozen of 'em – counting Sterndale.'

'I guess yuh don't count the gel,' said Lye Spar. Judson scowled. He didn't like being reminded of how Milly had run out on him, preferring the company of a bunch of outlaws to his own.

The posse split up again, and, taking different directions, speared into the hills. Judson's party picked up the trail of the fugitives, but lost it again in a shallow stream. They searched diligently until they suddenly ran into the other mob, who had doubled on their tracks. Trigger-happy waddies on both sides, thinking they had found their quarry, drew their irons. Bloodshed was averted just in time, but tempers remained very frayed.

For the second time, the hunters returned empty-handed.

'Never mind,' said Judson. 'We've got all the time in the world. Let 'em stick in the badlands. We'll get them sooner or later.'

The funeral of Sheriff Joe Budd was attended by most of the populace of Georgetown, including the Judson faction. The king-pin himself was at his ranch, the Cross M, but he sent a magnificent wreath.

Afterwards, young Oakland shut himself up in the bungalow. The tragedy had hit him very hard. His dad shot by his best friend – and he'd got nobody else left in the world, except maybe Mrs Lopez, the half-breed housekeeper.

But Oak, bone and blood of his fighting father, was not the sort to stay under for long. He began to make plans. He began to visit the sheriff's office and get things straightened out. Pretty soon he knew without question what he meant to do. He spent a hell of a lot of time in the office, and people began to speculate about it. They did not know that most of the time he was in there he was practising his draw.

He did a lot of riding, too.

He was sitting in the office one morning when the door opened and Mervyn Judson and Ralph Messiter entered.

'Mornin', Oak,' said Judson affably.

'Mornin',' replied the young man. He pushed his chair away from the desk but did not rise.

He slid the two guns into their holsters on his crossed gunbelt – a brand-new one. Messiter, the professional, watched him with a speculative glow in his eyes and a faint smile on his face.

'Sit down, gentlemen,' said Oak. He was very much at ease.

The two men drew up chairs on the other side of the desk and seated themselves.

Judson did not waltz around. He said: 'You've bin ridin' out quite a bit lately, so they tell me, Oak. 'Uv yuh bin lookin' fer sign?'

'Kinda.' Oak didn't think it necessary to tell them that all he went out for was to get a bit of target practice.

'Find anythin'?' said Judson. 'Any signs o' that bunch, I mean?'

'Nope. Nary a smell of 'em.'

'Looks to me like they've finally lit out altogether. I guess we've seen the last of 'em.'

'Maybe,' said Oak. But he knew Frank Carter and the Trouble J boys better than Judson did. He figured something was bound to pop again sooner or later. Maybe he'd get his chance then. He was biding his time.

'Anyway,' said Judson. 'I figure it's time we got organized. Time we got some more law in this town now your dad's dead.'

'I agree.'

'So,' continued Judson. 'I've decided to appoint Ralph Messiter here as sheriff. He's the best man to handle the job . . .'

'You cain't do that,' said Oak.

'Whadyuh mean, I cain't do it? I'll do as I damwell please . . .'

'Hold your hosses, Mr Judson,' said Oak. 'An' I'll tell yuh why you cain't do it.'

With difficulty Judson restrained himself. It was becoming increasingly hard for him lately to maintain his former poker-faced control. The Trouble J boys had shaken him more than he would admit and although he opined he'd seen the last of them he would have felt much easier had they all been wiped from the face of the earth. Now was his chance to assert himself, to strengthen his domination over Georgetown.

Ralph Messiter had not turned a hair. He sat immobile, his cold eyes watching Oakland Budd's every movement.

Oak said:

'Two days before Dad wuz killed he made me his deppity in place of Hank O'Toole.' He flipped back his vest. 'Here's my deppity's badge.' He unpinned it and tossed it on the desk. Then he opened a drawer and produced another silver star. 'An' here's the one I'm wearing in its place from now on.' He pinned it in a prominent position on the breast of his vest. It was the sheriff's badge his father had always worn.

Messiter moved slightly in his chair. His eyes met the younker's for a second. Then the latter's gaze passed on to the big ranch owner who was still speechless.

'Yuh see, Mr Judson, the sheriff's job is mine by right of bein' next in line – if you can think of any good reason why I shouldn't hold the job, wal, you can have an election. But I guess that's hardly worth while. There's no point in it – we're both fighting for the same cause. I want tuh get Frank Carter an' his gang jest as much as you do . . .'

Judson was flabbergasted, bowled over in astonishment at the gall of this kid, and yet, instinctively, already beginning to scheme. All he said was:

'You ain't old enough.'

'That ain't original, Mr Judson,' said Oak.

'Cut the cackle,' said Ralph Messiter, suddenly. 'I came here . . .' He stopped moving again in his seat.

Oak's hands dipped, came up holding two gleaming Colts. Nonchalantly Messiter crossed his hands on his lap. A little smile trembled on his thin lips, but his eyes were like ice.

'Kinda jumpy, ain't yuh, kid?' he said. 'I gotta hand it to yuh though. I didn't think yuh wuz that fast. Think you can haze me?'

'I hazed you that time.'

'Naw,' said Messiter with a shake of his head.

Judson looked from one to the other of them. His heavy face was in repose now, but there was a speculative glint in his eyes.

Oak said: 'Can yuh see any reason why I shouldn't hold the job? The ordinary townsfolk ain't gonna kick about it . . . All I want tuh do is get the people who killed my Dad . . .'

'All right,' said Judson. 'If that's what yuh want we'll let it go fer the time bein'. But watch yourself . . .'

'I allus do.'

'Boss . . .' said Messiter.

Judson cut him short. 'Come on.' He rose. Then he turned again to Oak. 'Yuh ain't got no reason tuh point them guns at us now.'

'No, I guess not.' The gib younker slid the weapons back into their holsters. 'So long,' he said.

To the decent townsfolk it would seem like he was throwing in his hand with the Judson mob and they wouldn't like that. Although they branded Frank Carter a cold-blooded young killer, a dead ringer for Billy the Kid, they inwardly gloated over the smack in the eye he and his gang had given to the Georgetown tyrant. . . . But, Oak reflected, his dad's mistake was that he had tried to fight both the lawless factions at once. His death was almost as much due to Judson as it was to the merciless younker who had pressed the trigger of the shotgun . . . Oak's mind echoed a phrase that he had heard his father use, 'my time will come,' and, even as it drummed at his brain another part of his mind was wondering what Judson had up his sleeve. Oak didn't want to become a scapegoat like his father had been . . . for a moment his face crumpled and he was a grief-stricken boy once more.

Outside, Ralph Messiter said: 'Why didn't you let me take him, boss?'

'Mebbe you won't have to,' said Judson.

So things moved gradually to their inevitably tragic conclusion, and down in the sleepy little border-town of Canon Pass the Trouble J boys prepared to ride once more. They had plenty of territory to cover so they collected a stock of provisions from Juan Consalez' little general store, Frank Carter, Lafe Kramer, Mel Sterndale, Big Bill, Dobson and Masters.

A girl in ornate but serviceable Mexican riding-togs came down the dusty sun-blazed street towards them. Blonde hair waved and glinted from below the wide brim of her sombrero. Her smooth lovely face was deeply tanned, her blue eyes shone as she stopped, hands on hips, and looked up at the men. There was a wicked-looking double-barrelled derringer in the belt which encircled her trim waist. She looked like a romantic, fighting frontierswoman.

She said: 'You're not leaving me in this pesky sandhole. If you're ridin' I'm comin' with yuh.'

'There's no place for a woman on this trip,' said Frank Carter.

'Yeah,' said Kramer. 'You'd better stay here, Milly.'

'Yes, stay here an' rot I suppose,' she said. 'I want to come with yuh an' help yuh.'

'Help us?' echoed Frank Carter harshly.

'I've helped yuh before, ain't I?' flared the girl. 'Why d'yuh hate me for it?'

'Frank don't hate yuh, Milly,' said Lafe Kramer. 'He . . .'

'He hates everybody,' flared the girl, her eyes blazing as she looked up at the youth in the saddle, his crooked arm in front of him, his eyes remote, unanswerable. Then she dropped her head suddenly, scared that she might reveal the sudden pity she felt. 'I'm sorry,' she mumbled. 'I didn't mean that. I guess this place is kind of gettin' on my nerves. I jest want to go with you. I ain't scared to take a chance. I know I can help you. If you won't let me come I guess I'll follow you, anyway . . .'

Kramer looked at the rest of the men. He looked at Frank last. The younker shrugged his frail shoulders.

Kramer said: 'All right, Milly. Get your tackle.'

The girl's blue eyes were soft as she looked up into his face. Did those hard, grey eyes flicker with a little emotion once more? Then the big man turned away.

'All right,' she said and ran back down the street.

'Wal,' said Kramer. 'I guess we'd better wait for her.'
'The gal's got guts,' said Mel Sterndale suddenly.

FOURTEEN

Night fell suddenly like a damp black shroud. It became hotter too, prickly and rough like a horse-blanket, irritating the skin and the nerves of men and beasts. Then the thunder rumbled and the first jagged lance of forked lightning split the skies apart, bathing men and cattle in a garish light, which vanished as suddenly as a snuffed candle, leaving the night blacker than ever by contrast.

The cattle, five hundred head of them, stirred like a sluggish mass of treacle. The Cross M night-riders gentled the restive horses and cursed the fates that brought them out on such a night. 'Melody' Trevenon, who had a voice like a nightingale and a heart as black and hard as ebony, began to sing an old border-ballad. The pure notes soared effortlessly above every other sound. The dogies forgot their panic and the steers gradually ceased their stamping and swaying.

But a deafening peel of thunder drowned the gentling voice and lightning slashed repeatedly at the sky once more.

To Melody Trevenon the thunder sounded for a moment like galloping hooves. He mentioned the fact to 'Limpey' Peters, who rode beside him.

'I didn't hear no hosses,' said Limpy. 'But mebbe it's some more of the boys comin' tuh jine us. I guess it's better to stick together on a night like this. Much more o'

this big-gun stuff an' we'll have a stampede on our hands.
Wisht it'd rain . . .'

Another terrific peel of thunder drowned his words and
lightning made everything bright as day.

'There is riders comin'!' yelled Melody.

Then blackness fell again. The riders were just vague
shapes as they came nearer. There seemed more than he
had expected to see.

'That you, boys?' he yelled.

'Take it easy, pardner,' somebody replied.

Then they were upon him. Like a rattlesnake striking at
the first hint of danger he drew his gun. There was a
boom, it seemed right inside his head, splitting his brains
apart. He knew no more.

'Hey!' yelled Limpy, swinging his horse. 'Help!' Then a
gun-barrel smashed on to his head and he toppled from
the saddle.

Lightning flashed again, revealing the tall form of Lafe
Kramer erect on his horse. His hand was pointing.

'Up ahead,' he yelled. 'Swing 'em. We don't want the
critturs to go in the wrong direction.'

He led the way as lightning flashed again, revealing
every one of the desperate band, and the girl who rode
with them. Four more night-riders turned at their
approach and began shooting: Frank Carter's shotgun
boomed and a horse squealed and crumpled. His rider fell
clear and rose, only to claw at the air and go down again.
His pards turned tail and ran for it.

The herd was moving now. The little band strung along
at the edge of them, riding hard. Every one but Sterndale
and the girl were experienced punchers. They were
approaching the narrowing head of the herd now and
were slowly, with gunshots and wild yells, helped out by the
thunder of the elements, forcing them over into the direction they wanted them to take.

The old leader-bulls were beginning to shamble

forward now. Pretty soon they would be in full gallop with the rest of the five hundred of the maddened herd streaming along behind them. And woebetide anything that got in their path.

'Over, you pesky critturs! Over!' yelled Big Bill Pretty. 'Hi! Hi! Hi! Yip – yip – hi! Oh – Oh Oh-Oh!'

The flanking leaders, terrified at the noises, began to force the middle bunch over – over . . .

'Keep 'em turning,' bawled Kramer. 'Keep 'em turning. Oh! Oh! There they go – there they go!' And, as if in co-operation the heavens opened up again and again and the mesa, the stampeding cattle, the speeding screeching humans were lit like a plateau in a fantastic nightmare.

One of the luckless night-riders who had fallen behind his pals got caught up in the front ranks of the speeding cattle. His body, a screeching waving mass of arms and legs, was thrown up into the air, came down again, then disappeared from view.

The cattle thundered on and on – over the rise – down the slope to the valley like a rushing, bawling rapids. The first ranks splashed into the yellow stream. Those who stumbled were trodden down by their fellows, who climbed over their backs and charged on. A quarter of a mile in front of them now were the Cross M ranch buildings.

The lightning flashed again and again. Then the rain began to fall.

The Trouble J bunch knew there might be other night-riders on the opposite flanks of the herd unless they had been unlucky enough to be caught up in the stampede. The two remaining men of the three that had bolted reached the corral before the herd caught up with them. Even then one of them managed to steer clear. But the other one was engulfed and smashed underfoot together with the wreckage of fences and other tackle.

The buildings were ablaze with light now and men were

scurrying around, some mounted, others on foot. The Trouble J boys swept down with the herd, firing as they came. Some of the Cross M men rode forward to try and turn the herd. They might just as well have tried to stop an express train with a full head of steam. Some of them paid for their foolhardiness with their lives, either knocked down by maddened beasts or by the bullets of the attacking force. The Trouble J boys were paying off old scores with a vengeance now. It was unlucky for the panicked Cross M men, many of them caught literally with their trousers down, that the driving rain, though lighting the sky and making vision better, made shooting difficult.

The charging steers found themselves baulked by the log walls of the bunk-house and ranch-house, though the latter's veranda and other flimsier stables and out-houses were smashed like matchwood by maddened beasts. They climbed on each other's backs in their frenzy at the obstacles which had stopped their mad rush. Some of them managed to get through and careered on across the range behind.

Men opened fire through the windows of the bunk-house. But the Trouble J men found plenty of cover.

The main mass of cattle seemed to be concentrating on the bunk-house now. Lafe Kramer and Frank Carter forced their horses through the milling beasts on the outskirts of the herd, and charged the ranch-house. No shots greeted them. They skirted it. The rain was abating as they did so. It stopped as suddenly as it had started. The heavens let loose a few more ineffectual drops then, as if satisfied with a job well done, closed up for the night.

The bunk-house walls were beginning to give way beneath the strain; from the shattered stables terrified horses milled with the cattle.

The rest of the Trouble J bunch began to skirt the buildings.

Kramer and Frank quickly hitched their horses to the

posts of the veranda and ran up the steps to the back door. It was bolted. They took positions each side of a window; with two vicious swings of the shotgun Frank smashed every pane in it and much of the woodwork too. They waited. Then Kramer dived through first.

Something scuffled in a corner of the dark kitchen. A deep trembling voice said: 'Don't shoot, baas! Don't shoot I's Mistah Judson's cook – he let's me sleep in here sometimes – I ain't gotta gun, baas, don't shoot . . . Nobody else here, baas, look – I'll light the lamp . . .'

'All right, Sam,' said Kramer. 'Do that – an' remember we got yuh covered.'

'Yah, baas.' A match flashed in a gleaming hand, lighting up a hurricane lantern on a shelf. The wick spluttered then blossomed into flame. Haloed like a phantom head was the glistening face and rolling terrified eyes of a negro.

'You sure there's nobody here?' snarled Kramer.

'Yah, bass. Sure, baas. Mr Judson gone to town.'

'You got a horse?'

'Yah, baas.'

'Wal, if yuh c'n find him get on him an' get away from here as quick as you can. An' don't go near Georgetown.'

'Sure, baas, sure . . .'

Kramer stepped aside. 'Git goin' then.'

The negro scuttled past him, cast a terrified glance at the other silent, warped figure, then dived through the window.

Kramer picked up the lamp and, followed by Frank, carried it into the living-room of the ranch-house. There he threw it into the middle of the thick carpet. The glass smashed, oil splashed. The flame flared and spread. They watched it until they were sure it had a good hold, until the heat stung their faces. Then they left the place. As they crossed the verandah a man came running round the corner. He paused, surprised, when he saw them. Then he went for his gun. Frank's shotgun crashed. The charge took the man full in the chest and knocked him backwards. Kramer re-sheathed the gun he hadn't had a chance to use. The two men forked their horses.

The rest of the Trouble J bunch were around the back now. Guns were flying through the doors and windows of the bunk-house and men were filing out through the back door with their hands up. Behind them the front walls of the bunk-house were beginning to cave before the onslaught of the cattle. Steers were coming around on all sides and charging on across the range.

Milly La Moure, her blonde hair shining as it straggled over her eyes, was gathering up guns and handing them over to her companions, most of whom were beginning to look like walking arsenals. The scared Cross M men milled in a bunch and cast apprehensive glances behind them. One of them suddenly gave a wild yell and drew a sneak-gun. Big Bill Pretty shot him clean between the eyes.

Cattle streamed past and fire spurted from all parts of the ranch-house and began to spread to the rest of the buildings.

'Where's Lye Spar?' yelled Kramer.

A scared voice said: 'He's only jest gone, Lafe. Ridin' tuh Georgetown to warn the boss.'

'Start tuh run, the lot of yuh!' bawled Kramer. 'Come On! Git movin'.' He raised his guns.

The Trouble J ranks parted as the Cross M bunch shuffled forward. Then the former began to shoot, ploughing up the ground at the heels of the retreating men. They began to hop and run.

'Faster! Faster!' yelled Big Bill Pretty.

'Keep 'em movin',' said Kramer. 'Get 'em goin' well. Then on tuh Georgetown. I'm off after Lye Spar.' He spurred his horse at a gallop around the corner of the buildings and on in the direction of Georgetown. He realized that young Frank was riding beside him.

'The crazy fools,' roared Bill Pretty. 'They'll go ridin' intuh town like that if we don't keep behind 'em . . . Come on, run, my beauties.'

Milly had already mounted and was streaming around the corner in the wake of Kramer and the kid.

Mel Sterndale, fearful for her safety, followed her. The rest of the bunch fired a few more parting shots after the Cross M people then leaving them to their own devices took to the trail too.

A dishevelled, wild-eyed Lye Spar burst through the batwings of the Curly Cat. For the first time in the experience of the people congregated there the snake-like little gunman seemed really beside himself. Judson turned from the bar and, at the sight of his man, his eyes started, his poker face crumpled. Something must be really wrong to get Lye in a state like that. The saloon-owner had a sudden choking sense of calamity.

Spar screeched: 'Boss – The Shotgun Kid an' his mob – stampeded the cattle – set the ranch on fire – they're coming here – behind me . . .'

Miraculously the saloon began to clear. The habitees had had one taste of the methods of that gang – they did not want another. Pretty soon all that was left were the regular Curly Cat gunnies and other employees – about ten in all.

Judson was cool now. Even the agitated Spar had calmed down.

'Out in the street,' said Judson. 'Take cover both sides.' He led the way.

He ran across the street as Lafe Kramer came galloping down with Frank Carter close behind him. Judson reached the opposite sidewalk. The majority of the Curly Cat bunch were in the middle of the street. It was Lye Spar who fired.

Kramer's horse screamed with agony. His front knees buckled then he went over on his side. His rider sprang free. Spar fired again. Kramer winced as a slug nicked his side. Then he was retaliating. Spar ducked to his knees. Other guns were levelled at Kramer.

Frank Carter swung his shotgun, discharging both barrels in quick succession. Three men collapsed screaming. The rest broke for cover. Frank jumped from his horse, ducked behind a rain-barrel on the sidewalk and began to reload.

'Rush 'em,' bawled Judson.

The Curly Cat men dodged along in the shadows, firing as they manoeuvred to get opposite the two men. The first gunnie to step off the sidewalk received a bullet in the throat from Kramer's Colt. But there were others behind him.

From behind the barrel Frank Carter's shotgun boomed and, as it did so, Kramer began to run. Another man writhed for a moment in the gutter then lay still. The rest of the Curly Cat people leapt back into the shadows. Then Kramer hit the boardwalk with a thud behind them. From there, as they whirled to face him, he began a sortie. Guns blazing he crouched a little as he advanced. Another man doubled up, clutching at his stomach and whimpering like a child. It was Ralph Messiter.

Lye Spar backed into the roadway, attempting to flank Kramer. Frank Carter fired again. The shot missed Spar but hit another man in the leg. He tumbled from the sidewalk like a maimed duck.

Spar and Kramer faced each other, firing simultaneously. Kramer staggered and clung to a post for support, still firing. Spar fell on his back, tried to rise, then sank back again and lay still. Judson ran into the street and fired at Kramer. The big man came slowly away from the post to which he clung; his fingers scraped at the wood, then let go. He fell forward on his face.

The Shotgun Kid was still reloading as he came out of cover. Galloping hooves told him that his men were approaching. But what he had to do was his job alone. Three men faced him now. One of them was Mervyn Judson.

Frank threw himself forward. He squeezed the trigger of the gun. As it bucked and crashed he felt a blow in his chest. He threw himself flat on his stomach, elevating the muzzle of the gun as he squeezed the trigger again. The smoke cleared, and through the pain that blinded him he saw that only Judson was left now and he was toppling like a huge tree. Frank watched his enemy crash forward on his face.

Frank rose to his knees. His men were here now. He heard Mel Sterndale shout: 'Get back, Milly, get back.'

Down the street in the other direction came a bunch of townsmen led by Oakland Budd. Frank raised his shotgun, then dropped it: it was empty! With his good left hand he tugged at the gun in his belt.

The young sheriff of Georgetown saw the movement and went for his own gun. But he did not need it. The Shotgun Kid suddenly rolled over on his side like a child going to sleep. He lay still, a crumpled forlorn figure.

Big Bill Pretty picked him up, light as a baby in death, and carried him to the sidewalk.

Mel Sterndale raised Kramer's head. Milly ran to his side and dropped on her knees beside him.

'Lafe,' she whispered.

'He can't say nothin' to yuh now,' said Sterndale gently.

It was early morning in Georgetown. Sunny. Gentle. Mel Sterndale walked down the street and stopped ouside the shattered front of his print-shop. As he stood there a stagecoach lumbered down the street in a cloud of dust and pulled up outside the Curly Cat. Sterndale watched it. He saw the lean old driver climb down from his box and go into the saloon, to return almost imme-diately with a large attache-case. He carried this around to the boot at the back and disappeared from sight.

Sterndale gently pushed the sagging door of his shop. It swung open. He passed into the dim, dusty interior. Shafts of sunshine speared through the broken windows, etched the rubbish and the destruction.

Sterndale rummaged around until he discovered a large, fairly clean sheet of paper. He took it over to the shattered table, which stood precariously on three legs.

He took a stub of blue pencil from his pocket and began to write in large block letters. An announcement: As soon as possible the *Georgetown Herald* would be in circulation once more.

A shadow fell across the sunshine. He looked up. Milly La Moure came into the shop. She said hesitantly: 'I've come to say goodbye. I'm goin' away on the stage.'

He held out his hand. She came forward and took it. 'Goodbye, Milly,' he said. 'Good luck.'

'Thank you,' she whispered. Then she turned to go.

At the door she turned again suddenly.

'Mel,' she said. 'Kramer . . . If he hadn't died – d'yuh think he would – d'yuh think we could've. . . ?'

'Yes, Milly,' said Sterndale gently. 'I think you could.'

She smiled. Then she was gone.

He went to the door and watched her get on to the stage. He waved as it passed him in a cloud of dust. He stood watching it until it was a mere blob on the immensity of the Western landscape.